Futurus Rex

Lynn Barker and D.C. Fontana

Published by Lynn Barker, 2022.

FUTURUS REX

First edition. July 18, 2022.

ISBN: 979-8201390389

Written by Lynn Barker and D.C. Fontana.

For Dorothy and Budd who believed in this story for so long.
-Lynn Barker

PREFACE

My dear friend Dorothy (D.C.) Fontana was always enamored of all things Arthurian; the equality of the round table, the story of a young, common boy destined to be king and the tales of betrayal by the adult Arthur's beloved wife, favorite knight and overly-ambitious nephew Modred. She loved the legend that Arthur would one day return from seeming death when he was most needed.

When our friend artist, writer/animator Budd Lewis brought us his version of Arthur's return, we were both intrigued and worked together to write a screenplay that was probably before its time in many ways. After Budd's death in 2014, Dorothy and I crafted the outline for a novel adapted from our screenplay. Dorothy wrote a portion of the novel, I wrote a section and, after her death in December, 2019, I finished the book.

As far as I know, this novel contains the last of Dorothy's writing that will be published. In "Futurus Rex", Arthur returns.... as she would have wanted.—Lynn Barker – July, 2022

Chapter 1

The moon rose slowly, its silver face reflecting back a double glow lighting the shining ring and debris belt floating in place around it. The light gently illuminated the bleak Earth horizon, touching the peaks of the mountains, gracing them with a soft glow.

Then the ring rays began to change, twisting and strobing queerly, turning blood red and reaching out toward the Earth below. In the stark landscape of that place, a strange stone ruin was revealed in a hillock's side. Fitted blocks, the remains of carven faces and ancient symbols graced what seemed to be a stone doorway fitting into the side of the hunched hill. It might have been a tomb once, or the entrance to an ancient place of worship.

The glowing red rays sparkled and throbbed with an otherworldly thrum that shivered in the air. Faint grooves in the frame of what once had been a doorway quivered faintly in the glow of the rays that slithered through a tiny slit at the edge of the door frame.

A vault lay behind the rock doorway. Long and dark, it suddenly glowed with the odd red light of the searching rays. Dark and silent banks of extraordinary machinery slowly came to life as long dead photo-sensitive panels began to illuminate, struggling to reinstitute the electronics they once supported. Switches clicked, and automatic systems snapped alive. Through a thick layer of dust, tiny lights flashed and illuminated the panels. A low hum accompanied the machinery that continued to establish itself.

Inside the huge chamber, the searching beam of crimson light came to rest on a dust-covered glass sarcophagus. The coffin was fitted with tubes, wires and hoses, all hooked from its base into the phalanx of machines around it. Some of them began to vibrate as they activated – and then the gem-shaped stone atop the sarcophagus suddenly lit up.

Light seeped slowly into the coffin, illuminating the tall, muscular male body that lay there. And then a long, deep breath surged through the body's wide chest.

After daybreak, at the edge of other ancient stone ruins, a sun-tanned, ten-year-old boy scampered happily around the tall, rough-shaped slabs, playing hide-and-seek with himself in the early morning light. Katch didn't need playmates; he had learned to create his own fun and games alone when he was a much younger child. He jumped as he startled a rabbit out of the cover of one of the fallen stones and then he laughed out loud. The rabbit bounded away, skittering from shadow to shadow, and disappeared down a grass-covered hole to safety. Katch carefully noted where it had gone. He and Aliena might want some rabbit stew some night. His beautiful sister was a popular songsayer with a lovely, clear voice and she accompanied herself with skill on the lyrit, a small, harplike instrument. She'd wandered halfway around the known world surviving as a troubadour singing songs of the legendary past. Music describing the oppressive, current rule of the Grand Magician Karayahn was forbidden but she had a few of those too. Aliena was very special. She could read and write and translate tiny ink dots on paper to musical notes on her instrument. Katch felt that she had seen and knew well....everything. And, she was home and singing tonight. He couldn't wait.

Suddenly, he heard a soft <u>swish</u> and then a gentle pop off to his left, over the slight swell of the rise there. Katch frowned. He had never heard such a noise before. He ran to the middle of the slope, dropped to his hands and knees, and crawled to the top, carefully peering over and down without raising his head too high. He caught his breath as a strange sight appeared at the base of the rise. What seemed to be a rectangular doorframe shimmered in the air. Suddenly, the space inside the frame began to throb with a glow of light; and a whining sound rose in the still morning air. And then, Katch blinked in disbelief and swallowed hard.

A very small thick-bodied man stepped nonchalantly through the shimmering portal. He wore an ancient-looking steel helmet and thick brown leather clothing which included a leather pack on his back. He scowled as he looked around the bleak landscape. Then he reached into his trousers pocket and pulled out a small, round, blood-red stone. He smiled mirthlessly and shoved the device back into his pocket. As he did, he turned toward the portal and impatiently gestured to someone.

"Come on, come on. Always larkin' about!"

The portal shivered again as another figure stepped through. It was a tall, very slender blond man who looked to be in his mid-thirties. He wore beautifully tailored clothes; a crisp white shirt under a well-fitting jacket of heavy cloth, tightly-fitted pants and high leather boots with the tops turned over to form cuffs at his knees. A sword belt and scabbard clung to his waist, carrying an elaborate-handled sword. A compact leather pack was slung on his left shoulder. He winced slightly as the area inside the portal gave a sharp snap and the light cut out when the door closed and disappeared, leaving the sky clear behind the two men. Katch's mouth hung open as he witnessed the weird arrival of these strange beings.

The little man shrugged and pulled a parchment from his backpack. He got down on his knees and spread the parchment on the ground, revealing it to be a map. The tall man stared around at the landscape while his companion pulled an odd-looking sighting instrument from his backpack, adjusted it and stared through the eyepiece.

"Nasty-lookin' country now. Used to be a sea out there." The little man gestured slightly toward the land away from the mountains.

"Where's Yaustis?"

The little man ignored the question. "There were cities once. But that was a thousand years ago."

His companion stepped closer, a look of concern on his face. "Tiberius. Didn't Yaustis come through the portal with you? I know I was a little late, but he should be here with you." He rapped his fingers on his sword hilt impatiently, waiting for an answer.

Finally, Tiberius grimaced and snorted in disgust as he got to his feet. "He's got his own plett. He can get through any time he wants." He tucked away the sighting instrument and reached down to pick up the parchment. "And if he ain't here by the time I roll up this map, I'm leavin' without him. Dumb dragon'll have to answer to the Council for it."

The tall man shook his head and stepped in front of him. "Yaustis is <u>not</u> a dragon. He's a thween and a highly regarded one. Why, his abilities to... "

Tiberius moved to the side, pointing toward the hill near them. "It's yonder, Padraig, m'boy. And a far way, too!"

Katch ducked low. He wanted to know who and what these people were, but he had to avoid being seen.

Tiberius didn't notice the small movement near the top of the hill. "It's a deadly haul to where we're headin', and I can't wait around for stragglers amongst us."

"The Council assigned Yaustis to this expedition..." Padraig began.

Suddenly, behind them, the portal whined and came to life. The framework opening flashed and expanded as a large, strange creature floated through gracefully. Padraig smiled and lifted a hand in greeting. "Yaustis!" Tiberius just grumbled to himself.

On the hill, Katch gasped at the sight of the creature. It was huge, generally round in body, covered in feathers resembling scales and with many small wings fluttering on it. Its long tail settled on the ground behind it. Its head hooked up on a slender neck. The head featured extra-large eyes that blinked accusingly at Tiberius and seemed to change color. Tiberius ignored it. Katch could hear a deep, pleasant voice, but could see no mouth at all.

"I had to pick the lock," the thween "said" while wiggling a claw on his forepaw.

Padraig scowled and took a step toward Tiberius. "You didn't give him his plett."

The small man shrugged and rolled up the parchment map. "Did so! Dumb dragon got no pockets to keep things in, not my fault."

"I do too have pockets," Yaustis said pleasantly. "You just don't know where to look and I'm not a dragon." He moved just above the ground with a graceful, swirling movement, toward the two men. His voice dropped to a whisper, directed to Padraig. "He's just piqued that the Mid-Eve Council chose a thween to lead the expedition."

Padraig shrugged slightly. "The point remains, they did choose you, not him."

Yaustis countered with- "He's still the best scout in the Enchantment. He knows this place. We do not."

Tiberius nonchalantly placed the map in his backpack and turned to the other two. "Don't talk about me like I'm not here! Yes. I know where I'm steppin'. Let's travel."

Padraig shook his head. "It's too dangerous to travel by day in the RealWorld."

"What makes you think it's any safer to travel by night?" Tiberius defiantly spit a gob to the ground and glared at them.

"Well... for one", Padraig responded, "we're from the Enchantment, and that makes us kin to the darkness."

Tiberius marched two steps to stand in front of his tall partner and glared up at him. "Padraig, there's boogers out here like you've never seen before. I've spent a lot of time scoutin' the RealWorld since the

Humans poisoned it with fire floods, and I've seen what growed out of it. Wait until <u>you</u> do. I say, travel and be danged."

Padraig looked at Yaustis. "What do <u>you</u> say?"

Yaustis fluttered his wings slightly and nodded his head. "We travel as we must," he replied mildly. "By day, we encounter Humans, and that's not good. By night, we encounter mutants, and that's worse." His head looked up toward the rise above them. "But to begin, we'll rest the day away up in that high meadow and begin our journey when the moon rises."

The thween moved slowly past Tiberius. The little man shrugged his shoulders and fell in behind the creature. Padraig shook his head, chuckling softly, and joined the strange procession up the hill.

On the hilltop, Katch gasped again as the strangers began to come his way. He ducked low and, knowing the path well, dashed quickly down the hill, through the ruins and away before they caught any sign of him.

Chapter 2

The Manor House of Bathlone Village was once a baronial mansion...a very long time ago. Large and three-storied, it had been built of local quarry stone. It still held the majesty of its original architecture, though the stone had suffered some cracks and chunks broken off from enemy cannon fire at one time. A strong gated wall stood around it, but allowed for crowds or teams, wagons and carriages in the large courtyard.

At this moment, mid-morning of a hot, dusty day, local villagers stood outside the wall, frightened, as they watched a troop of Garrum Guardsmen march through the open gate. The Garrum were all big. Helmets encased their heads and faces, allowing only their eyes to be seen which, to some, was a good thing since many were malformed mutants. Heavy black body armor covered their all-black uniforms, but allowed them to move fairly freely. They all carried swords and high-powered tech rifles. Garrum had already occupied the wall's guard posts as well and stood openly studying every questionable move the villagers made outside the manor house, not that the villagers made any. They understood a house under martial law was not to be approached unless the master issued an invitation. The master of this house was not about to do so.

Marshal Connery Beige sat in the dining hall, angry but hiding it reasonably well. While it was only nudging noon on the clock, the hall had been decked out for a feast, but few of the guests were in a festive mood. People in important village positions sat stiffly at the tables, clearly nervous and not in the mood to eat from the huge platters the busy servants set out on the long tables. They were made even more nervous by the armed Garrum lining the walls of the large room.

Beige felt the same way. A handsome man in his mid-thirties, he wore a formal uniform and was clearly uncomfortable in it. He kept pulling at the tight collar. His blond hair fell in a loose straight line across his brow and halfway down the back of his neck. Tall and strong-bodied, he filled the role of Marshal, but he hated it. He eyed the gross, mutant humanoid across from him with ill-hidden dislike. The Executive Officer, Mekahn, was oversized, like all Garrum, tall and broad with a bloated, warped face that almost swallowed the two black eyes with which he stared in amusement at Beige.

A joint of roasted meat from a large animal sat on a platter in front of Mekahn. He reached out, casually ripped a chunk from it and chewed on the yellowish meat as he leaned toward the man opposite him.

"Not hungry, Marshal Beige?"

Beige thought angrily that hunger didn't enter into it. Anger did. The Grand Magician Karayahn ruled the world, at least what most people here knew of it. The Garrum were her muscle, the enforcers of whatever she chose to put into law and Mekahn was the (really ugly) face of that law enforcement. Until Karayahn had taken power, the people of Gritania had been free to do the best they could to survive and accomplish their goals without too many squabbles...and no wars. The old ones remembered wars. Their forebears had told them all about them and they didn't want them. Which is why Karayahn had been able to seize total power so easily. No one wanted to oppose an armed force like the Garrum.

Beige hadn't wanted to be the Marshal of Bathlone Village...or anywhere. He had led a very different kind of life, until someone had reported on his (he scowled) "leadership abilities." Karayahn had instantly appointed him Marshal of the village.

Mekahn leaned closer, confidentially, ignoring the angry look Beige slanted at him. "Beige," he said around the meat, "just because the Manor House is under martial law doesn't mean you can't be a decent host. Set an example for your household and your guests. Eat. Or I'll have it forced down you." He swallowed the chewed meat in a big gulp and slanted a rotten-toothed smile at Beige.

Beige shifted in his chair and smiled tightly. "My apologies, Mekahn. Sometimes I forget my obligations."

Mekahn nodded, as if he really understood. "Yes, well, when one is not born to rank, good form is foreign." He lifted one eyebrow suggestively. "Perhaps you were better suited to banditry than to officialdom."

Beige again tried to force a smile, but failed. Instead, he reached for a small piece of the roast with his fork and ate it slowly. He wished he were still a bandit.

In the Manor House kitchen, tray servants, cooks and other kitchen help bustled about, busy but not enjoying the work. While there were no Garrum actually in the room, several could be seen through the windows walking back and forth in the service courtyard, on guard against any suspicious activity.

Uninvolved with the food and serving work, a lovely young woman sat in the corner, lost in thought and gently touching the strings of her musical instrument, a lyrit, a bit like a small harp but with a unique curved shape. Auburn-haired and green-eyed, she stood tall and finely built; but her long legs were tucked under her chair at the moment. Her clothes were clean, but simple; black, well-fitting pants tucked into tall boots, a soft, full-sleeved white shirt partly covered by a deep copper-colored velvet sleeveless vest that fell below her waist and was held in place by a wide belt with a silver buckle. On her wrists were two wide, black leather bands. Her long fingers plucked a soft, simple melody from the lyrit and she nodded her head to the tune of it.

Katch burst through the open door from the courtyard, excited and out of breath. He cast his eyes around the busy kitchen. The workers seemed to know him, as no one challenged his presence there or even spent more than a second eyeing his entrance. Catching sight of the young musician, Katch ran toward her, shouting.

"Aliena! There's monsters in the high meadow!"

The young woman snapped out of her musical daydream and turned to the boy. She smiled at him and shook her head. "Oh, and you're the only one who can see them, right?"

"Sister, if you want to see them, come with me now." Katch had turned and was practically poised on his toes to run for the door again.

"The only thing I want you to do right now is come hear me play," Aliena replied gently.

Katch's shoulders sagged, and his young face clouded. He glanced toward the door to the dining hall nervously. "Will it be all right? You've been away a long time, and it hasn't been easy for me around here since the new Marshal took over."

Aliena shrugged easily. "It isn't his fault the Guardsmen garrisoned the Manor House. If we don't fight them, they'll go away, and things'll get back to normal."

Katch shook his head, unconvinced. "I wish I was a magician. Then all I'd have to do is close my eyes..." He extended his hands and closed his eyes to show her. "Make a wish and say 'Go away!' and <u>poof</u>!" He opened his eyes and looked at her hopefully.

Aliena reached out to hug Katch, trying to laugh convincingly to reassure him. "Magic's not for people like us, little brother. Magic gives people too much power, like the Grand Magician. We'll just depend on happy songs, all right?"

"I guess so," Katch said uneasily. "But there really are monsters in the meadow."

Aliena adjusted her lyrit on her left arm and stood up. She smiled as she patted Katch on the shoulder. "There are monsters in the dining hall, and I've got to go sing for them. Come on, Katch. Sneak under a table and listen." Laughing together, they threaded their way through the busy kitchen toward the hall.

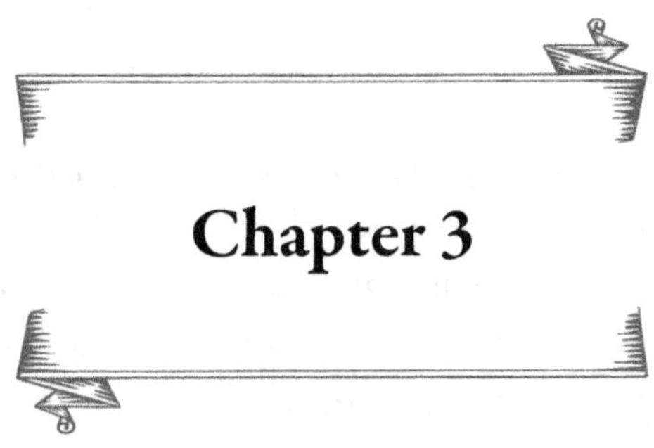

Chapter 3

In the vault, behind the stone door, a red warning light activated on one machine. Then a blue light, then a green one. Pressure valves instantly released and a long, low hissing sound issued from the sarcophagus.

The glass coffin lid began to open slowly. Centuries of dust obscured the coat of arms that had been engraved on the lid until it started to rise. Then the dust cascaded off, showering to the floor, revealing three gold crowns etched into the lid.

Inside the coffin, the man stirred slowly and painfully, stretching his arms and legs carefully. Finally, he seemed to gather himself and managed to sit up and look around blearily. There was a latch on the side of the coffin. When he pushed it, the entire side slowly lowered to allow him to swing his legs and feet out to the ground and slide to a standing position.

The three-crown coat of arms indicated this man was King Arthur, at the beginning of his long-prophesied return. Overhead lights blinked on, revealing the coffin as a cryogenic suspension tank. As Arthur moved carefully and a bit shakily around the coffin tank, his naked body showed him to be tall, muscular, still strong and apparently healthy. A bit of gray in his dark hair and beard set him still in his forties, and his light brown eyes glinted at the sight of the machinery that had preserved his life for centuries.

As he stood, slowly and carefully exercising his lungs and muscles, another light flashed on, just below the coffin/tank. Arthur bent over and began to draw out carefully preserved trousers, a tunic, boots, gloves and other clothing exactly his size.

It took very little time to don the clothes, but the rest of his exploration brought little but pain. Around the walls of the cavern were other cryogenic tanks standing upright, all connected to the great battery of machines. Each had a different crest of arms engraved on the glass of the front, but the tanks were dark inside.

Arthur pulled them open, one by one, each more disheartening than the last. "Gawaine... Gaheris... Percival... Bedivere... Tristan... Bors... Lamorak... Kay... Galahad...." Every one was filled with dust or a few bones... a sword or shield in one or two. Arthur paused in front of each in a moment of mourning recalling battles and times of rejoicing with each knight.

The final tank he faced still functioned. The crest on the glass showed three crowns with a black band sinister across it. Arthur stared unbelieving at the slumbering face of the young man in the tank...handsome, dark-haired with a moustache and pointed beard.

"Modred," he whispered hoarsely using his voice for the first time in centuries.

Stricken, he spun around, grabbing a sword that had fallen from Gawaine's tank and raised it to smash Modred's coffin. He was prepared to swing the heavy handle into the glass, but then he paused...and lowered the sword to the ground.

In a pain-filled voice, Arthur whispered to himself and to Modred, "Here am I, with all my best scattered about me, left with only you, my very worst." He took a deep breath, reached forward and released the seal on the front of Modred's tank. "Come then. Awaken."

As the tank revived him, Modred slowly stirred; and his eyes fluttered open. For a moment, he stared uncomprehendingly at Arthur, then he struggled erect and pushed the lid open, gasping for air. "You!" he hoarsely spluttered and croaked. "I thought I killed you!"

Arthur glanced around the chamber at the dust of his lost companions and nodded, grimly amused. "Yes. So did I."

Tray servants circled the tables in the Manor House dining hall, collecting the empty dishes. The platter in front of Connery Beige was untouched except for the tiny shred of roast he had eaten earlier.

Mekahn's plate had been almost licked clean. He tossed the last clean-picked bones onto his plate and shoved it toward a server. He eyed Beige's plate mockingly. "Excellent job, Marshal. It takes a real artist to rearrange a full platter so it looks like food's been eaten. Maybe you have the makings of a politician after all."

Beige smiled thinly, his blue eyes narrowed in tightly held anger. Mekahn belched loudly, rubbed his big belly and then slapped his hands together. "Now, do we watch dancers, or do we talk about the lack of tax tribute from your town?"

Beige straightened, his anger ruling his judgment. "Taxes? Listen, Mekahn, we've given your bloody mistress...."

"Ah, ah, Marshal!" Mekahn waved a finger in Beige's face. "Let us keep civil tongues and official thoughts when speaking of the Grand Magician."

Beige pulled his anger in and replied bitterly, "Right. Since Karayahn seized power, she's free to take whatever she wants. You Executive Officers see to that. If the Grand Magician requires more from Bathlone Village, I'm sure you'll drag it out of us for her."

"Indeed." Mekahn smiled broadly. "And now that we've talked taxes, let's see those dancing girls."

"No dancing girls," Beige replied. Mekahn began to frown. "But..." Beige gestured to a corner of the hall.

Aliena had been watching, carefully keeping out of sight until she was wanted. She saw Beige's sign and waved back. As she began to make her way toward the center of the room, Katch unobtrusively slipped in and wriggled under a table.

"But....?" Mekahn prompted impatiently.

"We have something to give freely. Something even Karayahn can't tax."

Mekahn brightened, a little curious. "What?"

"Music and songs to say."

Mekahn made a face and slumped back in his chair, unimpressed.

Beige continued, smiling at Mekahn's reaction. "Presented by the songsayer, Aliena, noted far and wide for her virtuosity as well as her beauty."

"Oh?" Mekahn brightened again. "Beauty?"

Aliena took her place on a stool set in the center of the room by one of the servants. Village guests recognized her and a swell of applause greeted her as she settled and looked around, smiling. Without being too obvious, she hoped to see where Katch had ended up.

Meanwhile, Katch had slithered under a long table, avoiding the assorted boots and shoes that edged it. When he reached the short end, he peered from under the tablecloth to see if he could spot Aliena, and was greeted by the sight of a pair of Garrum Guardsman boots standing there at attention.

Katch frowned angrily, shut his eyes, crossed his fingers, pointing them at the boots. Softly, he hissed, "Go away!"

The boots turned sharply and walked away as Katch opened his eyes. He grinned in triumph...but only for a moment as another pair of Garrum boots marched in and took up the position. "Change of watch," Katch muttered angrily. He stretched around to peer between the sets of boots to see his sister.

Aliena surveyed the assembled crowd and settled her lyrit in place to play. She strummed a chord and let it linger on the air for just a moment. "Dearest lords, cherished ladies," she began, "a song for your edification. A song of romance and dreams....said so because I can't remember who I swiped it from." A wave of polite laughter rewarded her sally. She strummed a chord again, a stronger, more melodious one. "It's an old tale, about the King Who Did Not Die."

Beige shot a glance at Mekahn, who had instantly frowned. They both looked back to the songsayer, who began her song.

"When he fell, they said he did not die. They said his men would with him lie. And while our world went on, our king would not be gone."

Mekahn's brows settled into a straight line. His fists clenched on two knives on the table. Beige noticed villagers were engaged and listening with interest. Mekahn was not amused.

"In all the years, while we fought and lost and won, they said our king had never gone. Beneath a mountain strong he lives, while we our all have given."

Aliena's strong, clear voice lifted the lyrics toward a final moment. Beige began to gather himself in his seat as he watched Mekahn's face grow redder and redder with anger. The Garrum was practically seething.

"When they say he died, we know they lied. He will return to us, for he lives on for us...Arthur, the once and future king!"

Mekahn leapt to his feet, shouting. "Enough! Arrest that woman!"

Beige was at his side immediately, trying to calm him. He laid a hand on Mekahn's, which still held a knife. "What's wrong? She was merely...."

Mekahn's voice rose sharply. "Treason! Her song is laced with it. Arrest her!"

Four Garrum Guardsmen immediately rushed to Aliena and seized her roughly. She was startled, but did not offer resistance. Her eyes darted around to land on Katch, under the nearby table. She shot him a look he read as meaning he should stay still and hidden.

Beige pushed in front of Mekahn, trying to bring reason into the moment. "I'm sure the song was innocent. Just an old legend. If you'll allow me...."

"Shut your mouth, Beige!" Mekahn shouted. "I still have wanted papers on you and every one of the cutthroats you ran with." He leaned around Beige. "Bring the traitor here!"

The Guardsmen dragged Aliena roughly before Mekahn and shoved her down at his feet. Mekahn grabbed the lyrit from Aliena's hands, and she let it go rather than harm it by struggling. "Please, Master," she begged. "Don't take my lyrit. It's all I've ever owned."

Mekahn shoved Aliena's shoulder, and she pulled back defensively. "You've turned it into a tool of treason. You sing of a warrior leader who will rise again to make the world as it once was. This is treason!" he shouted.

Beige heard a grumble of protests from the villagers around them, but it was almost drowned out by the snarls of the Guards. Mekahn ignored it and signaled to the Guards to drag Aliena away. "Treason is punishable by death."

Beige angrily grabbed Mekahn's arm. This was too much. "Not in my house, Mekahn!" he growled. "Not my subjects! Not on <u>your</u> authority. <u>Do you understand</u>?"

Mekahn paused, not only because of the murder he saw in Beige's eyes, but because he heard a soft murmur of approval from the villagers. He looked down at Beige's strong hand on his arm.

"Yes," he said sharply. "And I respect your position, if not you personally. Do <u>you</u> understand, Beige?" He flipped his wrist, releasing Beige's grip, and turned causally to his Guards. "Release her," he said quietly. "No blood will be spilt on my host's floor."

Aliena and Beige came together side by side almost accidentally as they stepped forward. Mekahn stabbed a finger at the young songsayer. "But understand this, Marshal," Mekahn, using his most officious voice and staring at Beige, made his pronouncement. "The jurisdiction binding this town belongs to me. Only me. This girl, innocently or otherwise, has said songs of treason in my presence." He stepped forward, his size menacing as he towered over Aliena. She shrank back involuntarily. Mekahn raised his voice. "The songsayer, Aliena, is henceforth exiled for the remainder of her life to the Outlands!"

Aliena cringed back, terrified. Under the table, Katch dropped his head into the crook of his arm and hid his eyes. Then he stretched forth his shivering hands, crossed his fingers and whispered, "Go away. Go away." No one heard him in the rumble of protests from the villagers.

Beige trembled with anger, struggling to keep control. Aliena meant a lot to him, maybe more than he'd admit to. Mekahn ignored him and lifted the lyrit, holding it out to Aliena. He raised an eyebrow mockingly and spoke in a falsely gentle voice. "When you again pluck its sweet notes, remember Mekahn and temper your songs with prudence."

She took her beloved instrument and was roughly escorted away. Mekahn grabbed a goblet from the table and glanced around the room. The low protest died away slowly. Mekahn raised the drink toward Beige mockingly. "Political office isn't the peach life of a bandit, is it, Beige?"

Beige's expression said it all. Not on your life, it isn't.

Aliena struggled in the Garrums' grip as they pulled her away. "Let me go! I have to get my things. I can't leave without my things…"

"Where?" a Garrum grunted.

"The kitchen. Please."

The apparent lead Garrum looked at the other over her head and nodded, one jerk of his head. They let go of her arms but followed on her heels as she moved toward the kitchen. She passed the table where Katch had scrambled out and stood watching fearfully. She shot a look at him and spoke loudly.

"May I leave a message for my brother?"

"What to say?" the lead Garrum snarled.

"That he should stay here, safe, grow up in the Manor House or at least in the village with people we know who will care for him."

The lead Garrum pushed her ahead of him roughly. "Should know that."

"But he'll never see me again!"

"Should know that."

"But...."

The lead Garrum, not one of the brightest, shoved her again, almost into the kitchen door. "Get things."

Aliena shot one final pleading look at Katch and pushed open the kitchen door. "It's just in here. Just a pack."

They followed her in, and the door closed, shutting off Katch's view. His eyes filled with tears.

Chapter 4

In the vault, Modred had almost finished dressing from the cache of clothing left in the drawer for him. He swung around to face Arthur. "No answers, my king?" He had to clear his long unused throat.

Arthur stood stolidly grim, watching his nephew complete his outfitting. "No answers, Modred," he said quietly. "Only more questions. The last I remember is facing you and inspecting your swordsmanship across my belly. I awoke here."

Simultaneously, they both looked around at the strange, still-functioning machines that had kept them both alive... for how long? For a moment, both stood silent in awe, then Arthur shook his head, considering.

"Merlin always said I would be the once and future king. If the past we remember is 'once,' and this is 'future...' am I still a king?"

Modred tilted his head, staring at him earnestly. "Do you want to be?"

"God... deliver me from another crown," Arthur said fervently.

Modred studied him carefully for a moment and sighed. "I have no desire for a crown either."

"I see," Arthur replied thoughtfully. "You did once... but not now?"

"I only want to know when 'now' is!" Modred snapped vehemently. "And find out why I'm here."

"Then for the first time, we are united in a common goal," Arthur said quietly. "Aren't we?"

Modred turned away briefly, considering their strange situation. Then he turned back to Arthur, squaring his shoulders. "Yes. You have nothing left that I want."

"What _do_ you want now?"

Modred laughed shortly, half-barking it. "No more than to survive. And you?"

Arthur considered it and then extended his hand. "A pax...?"

Modred stared at the hand he never thought he'd see extended in camaraderie and finally smiled, accepting it. "Pax! Is there anything to drink around here?"

The Garrum Guards marched Aliena out of the Manor House toward the village wall. Beyond the heavy gate lay the sweep of flat land with crops and pastures that led to the horizon where she would have to disappear from the most civilized and settled places. She had a heavy pack on leather support straps on her back and carried her lyrit, now in a protective case.

They reached the gate, which swung open on the lead Garrum's hand signal. They nudged Aliena forward to the outside and blocked her way when she turned to look at them. "Go."

"How can you know I'm going to the Outlands? I can hide anywhere," she cried defiantly.

"Sky fly," the lead Garrum said, lifting his hand to indicate above.

Aliena looked up and saw it, a small object hovering in the sky over her head. It shone brightly on its own power even in the afternoon sun.

"Sees you everywhere. All the time."

Aliena's shoulders and head drooped. That thing would follow her. She'd heard of them before, but had never seen one. Now here one was, watching her. Maybe forever. She nodded, turned her back on the village and began to trudge down the path between the fields toward the far distance that was the Outlands. The sky drone followed her for a time then seemed to short out, sputter and run out of power then fall to earth—useless. Aliena laughed. She'd seen yet another of Grand Magician Karayahn's mechanical marvels fail.

Arthur and Modred scoured the vault, searching for an exit. The structure was huge, carved out of the mountain's native rock but no doorways or entrances were obvious. Arthur jammed his fists on his hips and looked around at the machines and tanks that lined the walls.

"You know," he said thoughtfully, "as odd as all these mechanical things are, somehow I have knowledge of them. They must be the product of generations that came after us."

Modred continued poking among the machinery, but glanced back over his shoulder at Arthur. "How did they get here in our time?"

"We're not in our time," Arthur replied flatly. "It was Merlin's prophecy that I would sleep in a cave until the world needed..." he paused, and then cleared his throat "...a King Arthur again. And there were dreams." He paused again, thoughtfully. "Not so much dreams, but small bits of information about what has happened to Mankind since... our time."

Modred halted his search and turned on Arthur angrily. "I had no dreams. No information. What else do you know, Arthur?"

"I know now is the time to complete the story of Arthur Rex. My knights and I."

"No knights," Modred snapped. "They're all dead! No crowns. No advantages. Just you and I....that's all."

Arthur stared at him and then replied mildly. "Of course. Just you and I." He glanced again at the long dead members of his round table.

Modred subsided into a surly silence. They moved again, toward a darkened corner of the cave. A large trunk was tucked away in a natural alcove. Arthur and Modred looked at each other and raised eyebrows.

Arthur reached toward the lid of the trunk, clicked an obvious lock on its top and lifted it easily.

Inside was a treasure trove of armor, helms, swords and daggers. Modred immediately reached in, selecting a slim-bladed dirk and slipping it into the top of his boot. He began to test the weight and strength of several swords, moving them around in battle position. In a matter of moments, he chose a sleek saber, narrow but honed sharp – a blade befitting his nature. As Modred buckled the belt and scabbard around his waist, Arthur lifted a large-bladed long sword and judged its heft and balance.

"Maybe civilization has progressed to such a degree that weapons are unknown now," he mused thoughtfully.

"Then we come with the advantage," Modred smiled. Arthur glanced at him, and then he tossed aside the sword. "Nothing for you, then?" Modred said scornfully. "You're just being poutish because your beloved Excalibur wasn't left here for you."

Arthur swung around to face him, started to say something, but changed his mind. He took a deep breath and let it out slowly. "A sword like Excalibur belongs to a man only once in a lifetime." He leaned down to pick up the discarded sword and a scabbard that fit. "I will take this one. Wearing a crown can only teach a man how little he knows about wearing it."

He strapped the sword on with a few efficient moves. As he turned to scan the contents of the trunk again, he spotted a single metal rod, smooth and simple, set into a nearby rock formation. "What's this?"

He moved toward it quickly and pushed it like a lever. Immediately, a hidden door slid upward behind Modred, allowing a strange dim light to pour in.

"What in heaven?" Modred gasped. "A door."

Together, Arthur and Modred stepped forward, exiting the cave.

A strange landscape confronted them as they squinted up toward the crest of the hill behind them. The hill and the land they saw were lit with a dazzling array of colors from the setting sun. Without a word needed between them, they climbed the slope of the hill to the top.

The stark beauty of the countryside below was dazzling to the eye. Even as the sun slid lower to the horizon, the eerie, red-ringed moon with circling debris field had begun to rise into the resplendent sky overhead. Both men were astonished. What sorcery was this?

"Is this Britain?" Modred whispered hoarsely.

Arthur nodded. "It has to be. It's where they said I'd return."

"Then what the hell happened to it?"

Katch burrowed into the pantry corner where he had stashed his clothes and a makeshift travel sack. The cooks and bakers didn't mind lending him the little space he took up. All he had to do for food was stand near a cook top looking forlorn and one of the kitchen people would hand him something tasty to eat and a beverage cup. They all knew his songsayer sister had to leave him at the Manor House to earn her own living in the larger world. If she lingered in the village, she would have soon outstayed her welcome. She could only sing the same songs so many times before the coins stopped coming.

Once he had his few belongings and some necessities in his bag, Katch slung it over his shoulder. He had put on a hooded cloak and strong boots because he would have to walk. The outer door was on the far side of the kitchen, and he headed toward it purposefully.

The kitchen staff noticed him immediately and they knew he was leaving. Two cooks and a baker immediately went to shelves and the closet, ferreted out supplies and stuffed them in a bag. The chief cook took it, stepped in front of Katch and bowed as he handed the food bag to him.

"Safe travels, boy."

Katch nodded, tears glistening in his eyes, and bowed back. He couldn't speak, but the chief cook patted his shoulder as he headed for the outer door.

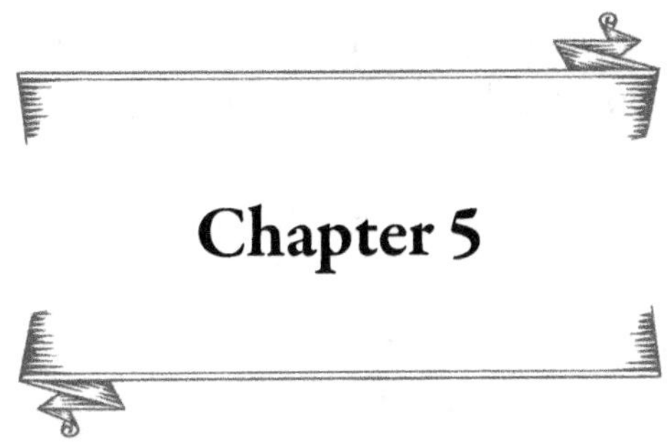

Chapter 5

The first story balcony stretched entirely around the outside of the Manor House. Mekahn strolled around it to the front, which overlooked the courtyard. He leaned on the banister casually as ten mounted dark-clad men drifted quietly into the courtyard. They stopped beneath the balcony where Mekahn looked down at them.

Further along the balcony, Connery Beige passed an arched door leading out. Spotting Mekahn, he stopped. Mekahn could not see him; but if he edged out carefully, there was enough shadow to conceal Beige as he observed the Executive Officer and the mounted Garrum below. These men were...different, an elite unit of some kind.

Katch, who had been just coming around the Manor House corner, heading for the main gate, heard the hoofbeats and slipped into the cover of the bushes that lined the side of the lower floor. He hunched down, pulling the hood of his cloak over his face and shoving his travel sack and food bag behind him. The horses had stopped almost exactly in front of him.

One of the horsemen, apparently the leader, looked up at Mekahn above them. "We received your signal, Master."

Mekahn nodded. "Sniff up the songsayer's trail, follow her into the Outlands. She is an enemy to Karayahn, and she is... a danger to me personally." He paused, then spoke more firmly. "Drian, Captain of Assassins."

The mounted leader, thinner than most Garrum but strong-muscled, moved aside the black veil he wore, revealing a dark mutant face. "Master?"

Mekahn made a little gesture with his right hand, waving his index finger. "Find her."

Drian nodded. "Execution, Master?"

Mekahn smiled. "Purely political."

Drian took out a laser gun and gave a military salute. Mekahn, satisfied, wheeled and reentered the house through one of the balcony doors. Drian covered his face again and led his mounted assassins toward the gate out of the courtyard. As soon as they were far enough away, Katch, more worried than ever for his sister, grabbed up his backpack and food sack and ran for the gate himself.

From a second floor Manor House room, Beige stepped out of the shadows to face the startled Mekahn. Beige's face had contorted in fury, and his fists clenched. "All those men to butcher one little songsayer. You son of a bitch."

Mekahn took a step forward to confront Beige. "Beige," he snarled, "those were your last official words. Consider yourself under house arrest."

Beige lunged for Mekahn, hands reaching for the Executive Officer's throat. Mekahn staggered back and shrieked, "Guards!"

Beige's fingers wrapped around Mekahn's neck just as the guards slammed through the door. They crossed the room in a few strides and grabbed Beige, hauling him away from Mekahn and pulling his arms behind his back. Mekahn instantly leaned forward and lashed Beige across the face with a closed fist. He snarled to the guards in a hoarse voice, "Take him below. Give him a lick of the Dragon's Tongue to relieve him of his position, officially."

Beige sagged to his knees as the guards roughly hauled him away. Mekahn watched them go and then neatly straightened his rumpled jacket, smiling at his handling of the situation. "Well done," he muttered to himself. "Very well done."

It took only a few minutes for the guards to haul Connery Beige to the jail cells under the Manor House. They handled him roughly, his knees and feet dragging and banging loosely on the stone steps. Mekahn followed several steps behind, smiling at the sight of the manhandling.

One of the guards hustled ahead with a torch. Reaching a barred door, he shoved it open and moved inside to light the torches there. The flickering flames barely illuminated the big, deep cavern but it was enough to show the wooden frame to hold a prisoner upright. The other guards pulled the semi-conscious Beige through the door and efficiently tied him spread-eagled to the frame.

Mekahn stepped into the vast chamber and approved the setup with a brisk nod. One of the guards moved to a chest in the corner, opened it and selected a slim rod. He showed it to Mekahn, who nodded again. The guard pressed a button on the base of the rod, and nine tails of laser light leaped to the end of it, dangling loosely. Mekahn nodded once more.

Two of the guards efficiently slit the back of Beige's vest and shirt with sharp knives, baring his spine. The whipsman stepped forward, raised the blazing bouquet of lashes and brought it down on Beige's back. The blow left nine slashes, deep and bleeding. Beige clenched his teeth and stifled a yell of pain.

The whipsman looked at Mekahn, who stood serenely contemplating the wounds. Since the Executive Officer made no move, the whipsman raised the laser cat-o-nine and slashed again. Beige gasped in pain, but made no other sound. Mekahn did not move, so the whipsman delivered another bloody blow to Beige's back. And only then did Mekahn raise his hand.

"No more. He doesn't need to die, just learn his place." He inspected Beige's back, noting the blood dripping to the floor and the smoking flesh. "He's thoroughly stripped of office." He gestured casually to the guards. "Secure him in his quarters."

Beige lay limp in the guards' hands, barely conscious as they cut him down and dragged him out of the dungeon. Mekahn dabbed a forefinger into the blood on the floor, admired it and laughed.

Arthur and Modred slogged through the night, wandering along a vaguely defined path. Arthur finally sighed and stopped. Modred pulled up beside him, looking around for anything that seemed like a sign. Seeing nothing significant, he turned to Arthur.

"What?"

"Two things I've noticed," Arthur said slowly. Modred arched an eyebrow, and Arthur glanced down at the belt buckle at his own waist. "We don't have any idea of where we're going."

Modred sighed. "And two?"

Arthur grinned and indicated downward. "And my belt buckle is winking."

They both examined the buckle, which housed an intricate device. The stone center actually did blink with a pale golden glow.

"What does it mean?" Modred asked.

"I don't know," Arthur replied. "But see...." He turned to one side, and the stone blinked in a slow sequence. "And now...." Arthur turned to the other side, and the blinking glow increased in pace.

"Can this device be playing 'Hot and Cold' with us?" Modred guessed.

Arthur shrugged and considered for a long moment. "Let's follow 'Hot,'" he suggested. He indicated the rapidly blinking direction.

Modred shrugged and moved after Arthur. They had only a barely marked trail to follow, but the light offered a signal, a way to go that promised to lead them...somewhere.

Hours later, Connery Beige stirred in the bloodstained bed in his quarters. Pain-wracked, he rolled onto his shoulder to the edge of his mattress and then eased to a sitting position. He took a breath and slowly moved his shoulders up and down, gauging the pain level. Deciding he could stand it, he got to his feet and surveyed his back in the large mirror over the bureau.

The lash marks had healed swiftly, but had left angry red scars patterned across his back from his shoulders to his hips. There was no blood, but the scars were deep and would remain to remind him of his punishment for the rest of his life.

Beige heaved his shoulders once, accepting the situation. He couldn't erase the scars, but they didn't have to weigh him down. He moved carefully across the room to the door and discreetly tried the knob. Locked. He paused a moment, considering, then turned and headed across to the chest at the foot of his bed.

It took a little effort to open the chest with his back as sore as it was, but he hoisted the lid finally. On top lay a folded hat, black with a peaked front and a handsome eagle feather decorating it. Beige pulled it out, straightened it and planted it on his head. He turned to the mirror on the wall and admired the hat as it decorated his longish blond hair. Pleased, he nodded and turned back to the trunk.

He discarded what was left of his Marshal's costume; the low boots, the trousers and belt. The chest held what he felt were his "real" clothes; a full-sleeved strong cotton shirt, a leather jacket, leather pants, a wide-buckled belt, cotton stockings, knee-high boots and a hooded cloak.

Once clothed, Beige took down a huge bow that had been mounted on the wall. Stringing it in one easy motion, he went back to the chest and removed another item. It was a leather semi-glove that he slipped over the top of his right hand, wriggling his fingers into the narrow sleeves and fastening it securely around his wrist.

Glancing around the room, his eyes centered on a plaque on the wall featuring the same symbol as the badges worn by the Garrum guards. He raised his right hand, aiming at the plaque, thumbed a small switch on the glove and clenched his fist. The gauntlet fired soundlessly, shattering the plaque into tiny pieces. Beige grinned and thumbed off the glove switch.

He turned to the chest again and pulled out an arrow-like device with strange electronic nodes attached near the head of the spiral shaft. He nocked it into the bowstring as he moved to the broad open window. Beige leaned back as he aimed the arrow high into the face of the moon, the action making him wince as the scars on his back protested. He paused a moment to consider what using this special arrow meant and fired it. Instantly, the arrow illuminated like a spiraling comet as it whirled away. Grinning, Beige shouldered the bow and climbed out the window.

"So long....and it's not been good to know you," he muttered as he climbed to the ground.

Like a lightning bolt, the arrow flew across the night sky, moving steadily north. Suddenly, a screech echoed nearby, and a fierce hunting falcon snatched it, ending its flight. Illuminated by the arrow, the falcon dove toward the earth like a falling comet.

Below, mounted on a horse, a teenaged boy looked up, startled. "Wolfer," he gasped in awe, "she caught a shooting star!"

The man named Wolfer, also mounted, glanced up and smiled. He was a tall, lean, handsome man, about thirty, his face decorated with a thin, dark moustache. His hat was broad brimmed and jaunty, his cloak and high boots were made of grey wolf skin. He extended his leathergauntleted arm, and the falcon landed on it with a fluff of its wings. The bird still held the lit arrow in its strong beak.

The boy stared at it, entranced. "I've never seen anything like it. Have you, Wolfer?"

Wolfer nodded. "The Calling Arrow." He took it from the falcon and then passed the bird to the boy. He nudged his horse and moved forward carefully to the edge of the cliff where he could see the glow of settlement lights in the distance. He swung the crossbow from his back, nocked in the arrow and fired it into the sky where it spiraled again in fiery light toward the settlement.

The boy moved his horse next to Wolfer eagerly. "It's the Foresters, isn't it? Calling each other together again?"

Wolfer smiled at him and stroked the falcon's head. "Take her home, Stoach. You and she are free of my service."

Stoach's bright grin faded. "But... why, sir?"

Wolfer looked up at the sky again. "It happens now and then, they say, on nights like this, when legends awake, and there's a red ring around the moon...."

Stoach, confused, looked up to see the moon had risen, silver and cold. Indeed, there was a wondrous red ring around the bright orb.

And the arrow flew on, flaring with light.

Chapter 6

In that rural town, a number of people walked the board sidewalks in front of the shops, a brothel and a wide-doored bar. Two rough-dressed men wandered idly by. Suddenly, a glass window shattered as three men spilled through it. Four more men brawled their way through the door.

The two passersby leapt agilely out of the way, just missing being hit by flying fists. "What's all that?" one yelled.

The other pulled himself together and shrugged nonchalantly. "Oh, just the old Foresters having a night on the town."

The brawlers hauled themselves up and went at each other again. Three were particularly distinctive. Jorn, a very tall, broad-shouldered, Nordic-looking man, was clean-shaven, handsome and wore his blond hair in a long braid down his back. He picked up a slightly smaller man in dark, non-descript clothes and tossed him into a porch post. A second man, Aaron, was also huge, but dark-haired and chocolate-skinned, dressed in thick brown leathers decorated with steel rivets and rings. He gleefully threw two attackers against the hitching post in front of the bar, startling a tethered horse into a neighing fit. Bishop Jobair "Jobie" Grey, a smaller man, held the title and could have been dressed as a holy man but his well-worn robes didn't identify him as such. He was beefy, but strong. He knocked together the heads of two shabbily dressed men trying to rush him. As they fell to the boardwalk, he reached down and deftly picked their back pockets, secreting their purses in his robes.

Suddenly, the Calling Arrow shrieked in and stuck, quivering and flashing, in a beam beside the bar door. Everyone in the area froze, staring at it. Aaron dropped the two new brawlers he had grabbed. Jobie dumped the man he was about to toss through an undamaged window, casually lifting his purse and stuffing it in his robe pocket. Jorn flicked his fist across a last attacker's face, knocking him flat. The Calling Arrow continued to flash.

A voice from the street called cheerfully, "There's a red ring around the moon." Everyone turned to stare at the young man of twenty-six standing there. Stellar Blue was of robust build, with dark curly hair that dropped to his shoulders, wore a blue cape and kid leather clothes and was armed with a short sword and a laser side arm. He raised his right arm and grinned broadly. "The Old Foresters ride again!"

Aaron, Jorn and Jobie cheered in response and began clapping each other's shoulders. The rest of the bystanders and some of the younger fight survivors, stayed silent and unsure. Who were the Foresters?

The Outlands Inn squatted alone in the desert, a long, low building with only its lights piercing the darkness. A number of horses, bare-backed, huddled in a nearby corral. Their saddles and bridles had been flung on the top rail of the pen to keep them out of the dust.

Someone came out of the inn, the open door letting some of the noise of the rowdy bar into the outside air. Aliena pushed past the departing patron and into the big open bar area.

It was filled with mutants of all kinds, all ugly and awkwardly built, but no Garrum. Several mutant barmaids threaded their way through the crowd, serving trays loaded with exotic drinks held high. Almost unnoticeable in the crowd were Padraig, Tiberius and even Yaustis, huddled in a corner of the bar making himself small. At first, the locals had been shocked by the strange creature's appearance but had gotten used to him. He didn't seem a threat and Karayahn's techno-wizards had created all manner of mutant creatures to serve her over the years.

As Aliena made her way through the huddled bar patrons, she passed Arthur and Modred, who stood at one end of the bar. Aliena had her eye on the innkeeper, Fanagan, who busily haggled over change with a mutant drunk. Fanagan was portly, middle-aged, with an ocular patch screwed into his left eye. The young songsayer slapped him on the back.

Fanagan swung around with an angry scowl, ready for battle. The second he saw her, his face contorted into a huge smile; and he opened his arms to give her a hug. "Aliena!"

Aliena hugged back fiercely, glad to have a friend in her exile. "How are ya, Fanagan?" She stepped back and looked him over. "Still haven't gotten that new eyeball you ordered, I see."

"Is that a pun?" the innkeeper responded with a grin. "Aah! You know how slow those damned caravans are. Can you stay?"

Aliena grinned and spread her hands. "When my stomach's empty and my soul's full of song, I always come here."

Fanagan slung an arm around her shoulders. "Sing first," he said, "Eat later. You get set up, and I'll quiet this mob down."

She reached up to give him a quick kiss on the cheek. "Just let me unpack the lyrit."

He raised a thumb to show his agreement. Then he pushed off among the crowd toward a raised section of the floor that served as a makeshift stage.

At the near end of the bar, Tiberius, Padraig and Yaustis munched food from several pans laid out before them. Yaustis kept all his wings still while Padraig unobtrusively fed him through a barely noticeable opening in his lower facial area. They took their time eating, not calling attention to themselves, but casting curious looks at the two men at the other end of the bar.

"They're not from here," Tiberius whispered to Padraig.

The tall elf shrugged. "Neither are we."

"Well, I've been here before," Tiberius pointed out. "They're just... really different."

Padraig looked around, eyebrow arched. "And so are we. Your point?"

"Keep an eye on 'em is all." Tiberius slipped a portion of biscuit with a slice of meat on it into Yaustis's feeding hole. "And keep this one fed." As Yaustis munched, his eyes seemed to change color from a light blue to a warm yellow...his equivalent of "Yum".

Modred's eyes darted over the crowd, taking in the mutant faces and other odd beings around them. That large... <u>thing</u>... at the other end of the bar was not comprehensible in his known world. But, he had to acknowledge, his world and Arthur's had changed. They had to accept what was, here and now, whether they understood it yet or not. Arthur's belt buckle had stopped blinking but glowed with a steady yellow light.

"According to that thing, we must have arrived at an intended destination", said Mordred glancing at the buckle.

Arthur looked around, knowing somehow that Modred was correct but, as yet, not understanding why.

A serving boy moved toward them and stopped expectantly in front of Arthur. "Somethin' for you, sirs?"

"Ah... some food?" Arthur's belly had begun to rumble some time past, but there had been nothing to eat in the cave, and this inn was the first place they had reached that could provide. Some roast venison would go down well, he thought.

"Kythe and fassle for you, then?" the boy replied casually.

Modred leaned forward, curious. "Kythe?"

The boy shrugged. "Y'know. Chopped desert eel fried in its own jellied fat."

Modred and Arthur exchanged startled glances. Desert eel? Arthur felt his hunger abate almost instantly. "Perhaps just some bread," he said. He pointed at a tankard on the bar. "And some of that."

The boy glanced at the mug and snorted. "Fassle. I offered you that in the first place." He stamped away abruptly, clearly irritated by the two ignorant oafs.

Modred shot a look at Arthur, suddenly concerned. "Ah... how do you plan to pay for this?"

Arthur poked his hand into a small sack hooked onto his belt and pulled out several gold coins. "It was left in the cave with some other personal belongings of mine."

Modred took a coin from Arthur's palm and scrutinized it. "I've never seen anything like this. Is it good coin?"

Arthur shrugged. "Gold is gold, is it not?" He glanced around to indicate the oddness of their surroundings. "I suspect not too many here question gold."

Modred nodded and handed the coin back to Arthur. "Let us try to spend wisely. If that is all we have, and there is no one waiting to pay you tribute."

"That being the case, we might have to work for pay."

The serving boy came back then, bearing a tray with a plate full of bread and butter and two tankards. "Bread and fassle." He plopped the try down on the bar, took the coin from Arthur's hand and walked away.

Modred watched and saw the boy was not coming back with change. "Work for pay. Interesting concept." He glanced at Arthur with a sardonic smile. "Especially for you my King."

On the opposite end of the bar, Yaustis turned his gaze from Arthur and Modred and scanned around the room. His eyes, now light blue again, paused on a black-cloaked and hooded man seated at a table in a far corner. The high collar on his cloak masked the bottom of the man's face, but his dark eyes were fastened ominously on Arthur and

Modred, studying their every gesture. Suddenly, his gaze shifted, locking deliberately and directly on Yaustis.

Yaustis wheeled around to the bar, wildly embarrassed. Trying to get Padraig's and Tiberius's attention, he hissed loudly. And then he hissed again. "Pssst! HssssssTH!"

Tiberius glanced at him, eyebrow raised. "Are you hissing?"

Yaustis leaned close and whispered. "Lower your voice."

Tiberius dropped his voice level an octave, but did not whisper. "Are you hissing?"

Yaustis shot a glance around warily and leaned even closer to Padraig and Tiberius. "Something's going on here."

"Yeah," Tiberius agreed. "The girl's going to sing."

Yaustis and Padraig turned and looked toward the center of the room. Aliena sat on a table, tuning her lyrit. A closer examination would reveal an intricate symbol which decorated the wooden tuning head of the instrument. Aliena tried a few chords and was satisfied. Softly, she began to play an introduction.

Fanagan took that as his cue and stepped in from the side, holding up his hands for attention. "All right, folks!" he began. "Most of you know her and if you don't, you've heard of her. Aliena the Songsayer!"

A patter of applause moved through the room. Aliena nodded and smiled to acknowledge it. She strummed a dramatic chord. "We've all heard the songs and tales of the Outlands."

The applause got louder, some people pounding fists on their tables and some whistling shrilly. Aliena smiled and nodded again. The room was hers, at least for the moment.

"Remember the tall archer, Dick Crimson, who played a longbow the way he played a lyrit?" She struck another chord as the room applause and whistles rose again. "I'll sing you one of Dick's old songs, one you'll remember...."

"A Star to Steer By!" one of the mutants shouted.

Aliena smiled again. "Aye. "A Star to Steer By." She strummed the intro, and her strong voice began. "Oh, give me a star to steer by, a cause to die for, a love to win. And I will seek the sky."

Her voice could be heard softly outside the inn where Mekahn's assassins reined in their horses. "Hope springs in a rebel's breast, knowing death is near, but fighting on to win a free man's grave."

Drian dismounted and bent low to the ground, almost as if smelling the soil. "Life limps on for those he's left behind." Drian straightened, looked at the main inn door and nodded to his men.

Aliena's voice was clear in the quiet outside the inn. "We'll meet another time, another life, where secret lovers dine."

Inside, Arthur leaned toward Modred. "It's a hopeful song."

"Except for the cause to die for."

Arthur quirked an eyebrow at him. "I might believe in it but I don't sing about it."

Aliena continued the verse, her fingers building chords to strengthen the words. Arthur listened. He liked the song and, he had to admit that he was attracted to the singer. "War lingers on. Its roots grow deep in space, inspired and fed by hate. We will be free..."

Some of the patrons turned and looked as the black-clad men entered, glanced around and began to slide through the crowd. Aliena frowned as she spotted Drian in the lead. "The rebels' cry is strong. For them, this dream. Together they'll carve a place..."

Arthur noticed and nudged Modred, nodding in the direction of the strangers. Modred pursed his lips. "Elite assassins."

"How do you know?"

"They're my kind of people."

Arthur snorted derisively, his hand dropping casually to the hilt of his sword, and glanced around again. He paused, noticing that the hooded man in the rear had straightened, watching the black-clad men edge their way through the mutant crowd. The Hooded Man rose slowly, putting his hands under his cloak, ready for what might happen.

Aliena's voice lifted over the rising murmur of the crowd. "Destiny they will create. The time has come; the force of peace has won!"

As the assassins moved further into the room, Tiberius straightened and nudged Padraig. "Uh oh," he breathed softly. "Get your sword out, Paddy. I smell trouble."

Padraig had already noticed the invaders as well and automatically reached for his sword. Yaustis craned his neck around and blinked nervously.

Drian suddenly looked toward the center of the room. Aliena acknowledged scattered applause and slung her lyrit on her back, slipping gracefully off the table. Drian instantly pointed his right arm toward her; a throwing dart flashed from his sleeve. A waiter unexpectedly stood up in front of Aliena, and the dart buried itself in his back instead of her chest. The man collapsed, falling forward at Aliena's feet as she backed away, startled. People began to scream.

"They're after the girl!" Arthur shouted.

The Hooded Man threw open his cloak, revealing a silver chainmail shirt and a utility belt holding various weapons and pouches. In response, Drian flicked his left wrist, making a glowing light rod appear in his hand.

"Powerhead!" Tiberius shouted to Padraig. "If it touches anything, the head explodes like a bullet!"

Padraig nodded, raising his sword and moving forward. At the same moment, Arthur threw himself into the crowd, fighting his way toward Aliena. He dived over a table, colliding with her, pulling both of them to the floor.

Drian pointed the powerhead at Aliena. The Hooded Man tossed a silver sphere into the air, above his head. It paused a split second, then suddenly shot out mace-like points. The Hooded Man gestured to the orb, and it shot away toward Drian, who had no time to dodge. The orb slammed into the assassin's hand, and he shouted in pain. The powerhead hit the floor, and the resulting loud explosion scattered screaming mutants in all directions. Confusion ruled the inn. Tiberius, Yaustis and Padraig plowed into the crowd, moving toward Arthur and Aliena.

Arthur pulled the songsayer to her feet; but as he looked up, another assassin moved in front of them, a powerhead raised and poised to strike. Aliena brought up her arm in a fist-fighting position and made a slight motion. Instantly, a whirling laser knife activated from the leather bands at each wrist, throwing blinding electronic light around her fists. She raked the right spin laser across the assassin's chest; and he fell, screaming and spouting blood. Arthur quickly marveled at both the girl's fighting skill and yet another strange new weapon.

Padraig rushed in and shouted to be heard over the crowd noise. "Get her outside!"

Arthur shot a glance around. "Where then?"

Aliena pushed between them, shouting, "I know a place! Follow me!" She took off, shoving rudely through the crowd. Arthur and Padraig glanced at each other and then had to sprint to keep up with her. Another assassin stepped in her path. She brought up her fists, and a red glare erupted in his face. He doubled over, screaming, as the laser spin wheels gutted him.

Arthur shot a glance at Padraig. "We'll have to thank her for rescuing us like this."

Without a hint of sarcasm, Padraig snapped, "She's got my gratitude."

As they pushed forward, bodies flew across their path, fists flew in every direction and the scream level rose higher. Tiberius came up to Modred, who stood silently watching Arthur's progress. Suddenly, another assassin rose behind the Hooded Man, ready to run him through with a sword. Tiberius snatched a tankard off the bar and hurled it at the assassin, striking him in the side of the head. The assassin sagged off to the floor. The Hooded Man had heard the tankard hit, and he turned to note Tiberius's position and that he had been the source. He waved his thanks to the little man.

Tiberius turned to Modred, who had not stirred. "Come on, slicker!" he shouted. "You've got a sword. If you're goin' along with everybody else, you'd best use it!"

Modred suddenly moved, adroitly pulling his saber from its scabbard and seemed to lunge at Tiberius. The elf ducked, but Modred's stroke was over his head and stabbed another assassin in the throat. The assassin dropped soundlessly.

Tiberius looked at the body and grinned. "They must teach some fancy swordplay where you come from, Ace."

Modred tipped his saber at him. "My friend, where I come from, they invented it." With a silent consenting look, they both turned and began shoving their way toward the door after Arthur and the others.

Arthur, Padraig and Aliena paused at the door and looked past the shouting, brawling mutants around them. Tiberius and Modred fought to the exit, tracked by Yaustis who knocked a few assassins aside with his strong tail. "Get goin'!" Tiberius shouted. "We're right behind you."

There was a moment of confusion as they all converged. And then, Drian's cold voice cut through the chaos. "Leave the woman here."

They swung around to see Drian and his five remaining assassins in a half-circle behind them. Their weapons were drawn, and Drian cradled his mangled left arm in his right. Around them, the brawls stopped; and a rough quiet descended.

Drian pointed a finger at Aliena. "This woman is an outlaw. By order of Executive Officer Mekahn and the wish of the Grand Magician, she is to be executed." He took a deep breath and then said, "Stand away from her, and you will be spared."

Arthur resolutely stepped forward to stand in front of Aliena. The others pushed a little closer in support.

Drian shook his head, but not one bit sadly. "Then let all eyes witness the will of the Grand Magician."

"Stop!"

The assassins turned, startled. Aliena gasped.

Katch stood on a table at the rear of the inn. His arms were raised in the air, commanding attention. His tear-stained face was dirty from his travels, and his cloak and hood were smudged and torn. His travel sack hung on his shoulder, and he was clearly unarmed. He was only a terrified young boy who dared to command murderers to cease.

"You can't kill my sister!" he shouted. "It's not fair. She didn't do anything! She <u>sang a song</u>!"

There was an instant of silence, and then Drian laughed. He and his assassins turned again toward Aliena.

"Listen to the boy," said a strong yet quiet new voice. The assassins snapped around again toward Katch.

The Hooded Man stood on the table behind the boy, his arms raised. Power radiated from him; he looked eight feet tall...and dangerous. "It wouldn't be fair to kill the girl or her friends. They are still innocent. By tomorrow, when they have truly become enemies of evil, you won't be able to kill them..."

Two of the assassins began to advance determinedly toward the Hooded Man, but they stopped when he suddenly gathered Katch up in his left arm and made a sweeping gesture with his right. As his arm came up, a blinding wind exploded glass and debris in through the windows, howling madly. Everyone in the room ducked and covered their eyes.

"...because you'll be beyond caring," the Hooded Man concluded.

As the assassins cowered in front of the magical wind storm, Arthur firmly took Aliena's arm and pulled her with him through the exit door. The others quickly followed, except for Modred, who hung back a moment to watch the Hooded Man's storm. As he turned and pulled the door closed behind him, the windstorm inside was suddenly joined by blowing rain and lightning.

Katch looked up at the Hooded Man admiringly, but then he saw the storm-hindered assassins pull out arrowlock launchers, guns that fired flaming arrows. The arrowlocks sprayed their missiles around the room indiscriminately, sending everyone to the floor for cover and setting fires in the walls.

Outside the inn door, Aliena struggled against Arthur's grip as new screams and lightning flashes came from the interior. "Let me go! That's my little brother in there!"

Arthur held her firmly but without exerting any pain to her arm. In his kindest, most reassuring voice, he said, "I believe your brother is in excellent and safe hands. Come... <u>now</u>. You said there was a place."

Aliena looked into his intense brown eyes for a long, painful moment. Then she sighed and led the odd little group into the night.

Chapter 7

Inside the Outlands Inn, the storm continued. The Hooded Man threw lightning bolts from his fingertips at anyone with an arrowlock in his hands. Katch wriggled in his arm, delighted. He pointed at an assassin attempting to sneak up on them from the side, arrowlock raised.

"There's one!"

The Hooded Man instantly shifted his gaze, saw the attacker and fired a lightning bolt at him. The assassin, struck in the chest, was slammed back, the arrowlock flailing wildly as the man was ripped apart. Suddenly, everything went still, except for the sound of the falling rain.

The assassins all lay dead. Slowly, people began to get up and move around as the lightning stopped. The rain did not cease as it put out fires, but the wind died away. The Hooded Man put Katch down, lowering him from the table to the floor. Then he stepped down himself to stand beside the boy who looked at him with stars in his eyes.

"You're really magic, aren't you?"

The Hooded Man smiled, just a twitch of his mouth for a moment. "Oh, no more so than a summer storm."

"But you can make it happen <u>inside</u>," Katch said with wonder.

The Hooded Man shrugged, again with a twitch of a smile. "That's not the hard part. It's much more difficult making it go away. Want to help me?" Katch nodded eagerly, and the Hooded Man put his hands up. Katch instantly imitated him. "Now, just wish with all your might and say..."

Katch closed his eyes, crossed his fingers and spoke with all his heart. "Go away!"

The rain slowly stopped. A few droplets remained, spattering into the pools on the floor, falling from the overhead beams. Katch slowly opened his eyes, amazed. "It worked."

The Hooded Man laid a hand on Katch's shoulder. "Well, my young apprentice, don't you think we'd best be finding your sister and her friends?"

"Yes," Katch said enthusiastically. "And do y'know something? Those three creatures, I've seen them before. But I don't know the other two."

The Hooded Man gave him a smile then, wry but genuine. "I do." He opened his cloak and looked down at a belt buckle like the one Arthur now wore. The stone blinked constantly.

A desert wash provided shelter for the moment. Overhanging rocks blocked some of the moonlight, but enough crept into the wash to provide a little light. Tiberius and Padraig, swords drawn, stood ready inside the wash, but peered alertly into the night. Yaustis moved about slowly, small wings fluttering, his eyes evolving from blue to a pale red indicating his level of anxiety. Modred perched on a rock, with drawn sabre, but his eyes moved from one to the other and toward the strange dragon creature sizing them all up carefully. Arthur stood quietly, listening to night sounds for anything out of order. His belt buckle had begun blinking again. Aliena crouched near the wash's opening, fingering her lyrit case, clearly agitated.

Tiberius edged closer to Padraig, not bothering to lower his voice. "I think they'll follow us. Don't you think they'll follow us?"

Padraig ignored the comment. "I wonder who that hooded man was?"

Tiberius shrugged it away. "I don't know, but he was working real flat-out magic."

Arthur heard, but no one else did as Modred muttered, "Familiar magic, I'd say." Arthur shot him a look. Modred noticed and shrugged casually.

Aliena suddenly straightened, slinging her lyrit on her shoulder. "I'm going back to find my brother," she said sharply.

Modred unfolded himself from his rock seat. "No need."

"What?" Aliena turned to him, non-plussed.

Katch suddenly burst through the wash's opening and hurled himself at his sister, shouting her name. Aliena caught him and pulled him into a loving embrace. "You rascal," she scolded, only half-meaning it.

Katch looked up at her imploringly. "You're not mad 'cause I followed you, are you?"

"I'm just glad you're all right." Aliena hugged him again tightly, then looked into his eyes. "What happened at the inn?"

"The magician killed the assassins with lightning. <u>Real</u> lightning!" Katch glanced around then and froze when he saw Yaustis, Tiberius and Padraig. He yanked at Aliena's sleeve and pointed at the outsiders. "They're the monsters that were in the high meadow!"

"Well!" Yaustis sniffed, offended.

Tiberius stepped forward, slapping his hand on his sword hilt angrily. "Monsters, is it? If that don't tear it....

And then, suddenly, the Hooded Man moved into the wash, commanding their attention. He spoke quietly into the startled silence. "Katch, there's only one kind of monster in this world, those of evil minds and cruel hearts." Was his glance at Modred intentional?

Arthur strode forward, crossing to the Hooded Man and stopping in front of him. "My teacher, when I was the boy's age, said as much to me." He dropped his voice and looked the Hooded Man in the eyes. "Merlin." Then, glancing toward Aliena. Had she heard? "uh, Merle".

Merlin smiled and leaned forward to embrace him. "My boy."

Arthur returned the hug, but a frown wrinkled his brow. "You've got a lot of explaining to do, you old fox." He drew back and frowned at his former counselor.

Merlin stepped back and nodded. "It's time."

"I'm sure," Arthur said. "But time for what?"

Merlin pushed back his hood, revealing the dark hair, dark eyes and lean intelligent face Arthur had known all his life. The magician was ageless. Merlin gestured at Aliena, who stood at the back of the group with Katch. "Perhaps the songsayer can acquaint you with the current situation." He paused for a significant beat. "And Karayahn."

Aliena moved forward to join Arthur and Merlin. Her brow furrowed in confusion as she asked, "Who doesn't know of the dark sorceress Karayahn?"

Arthur gave her a half-smile, designed to encourage her to give more information. "I for one," he said. Then he added mildly, "I come from a far place."

"Very far," Aliena said skeptically, "not to have heard of her." <u>Who is this one</u>? Was the clear look on her face.

"Tell your tale, child," Merlin urged gently.

Aliena shot him an arch look, but shrugged. "Twenty-four years ago," she began, "Karayahn created an army of mutant soldiers and renegade techno-wizards and made war on the benevolent Aregnan princes who ruled us. The Aregnan family were all murdered, and Karayahn began her dark rule."

She stopped abruptly, and both Arthur and Modred looked at her sharply. "Something you are leaving out?" Arthur asked.

Aliena hesitated briefly, then said softly, "It's said there's a rebellion gathering against Karayahn and her Garrum army, but it needs a military leader to give it an even chance of success."

Arthur turned and stared squarely at Merlin. The old wizard smiled knowingly. Arthur braced himself against the sudden knowledge of why he was "reborn." A new battle, a new quest, a much altered realm. "I see," he said softly.

Merlin took in a deep breath, satisfied. "I thought you would."

Aliena heard the soft interchange and took a step toward Arthur. "Do you know a military leader who could help the resistance?"

"Well, I once had the title of 'Dux Bellorum,'" he said, his chin lifted in pride.

Tiberius pushed forward. "Duke? The man's a duke?"

Arthur turned toward him, shaking his head. "No. I am called..." he paused and then recovered "Artos. My mother was Duchess of Cornwall, but I am not a duke."

"You just said you were called Duke Bellorum," Aliena snapped and placed her hands on her hips. "Are you a duke or aren't you?"

Arthur blinked and tried for a reasonable answer. This beautiful girl reminded him of his feisty, long ago queen. "That title simply meant I was a war leader once." He turned to Merlin. "Eh... Merle?"

Merlin smiled and shot back, "And will be again?"

Before Arthur could answer, Yaustis fluttered his way close to Merlin. "Can techno-wizards open portals?"

"Portals?" Merlin asked, confused at the seemingly unrelated question from this extraordinary being. "What do you mean?"

Both Tiberius and Padraig turned to Yaustis. The large creature fluttered forward to face Merlin. "Permit me," he said courteously, his eyes back to their soft blue. "I am Yaustis, a thween, and leader of an expedition to these lands." He nodded to indicate Tiberius and Padraig. "Yonder is General Padraig of the Gentry. And Tiberius, our worthy scout and guide." Each bowed slightly at mention of his name. Yaustis resumed his flutter. "We come from the Enchantment....in elder terms, the Land of the Fae."

Tiberius chipped in pertly. "Y'know... elves and trolls, fairies and such."

"But that can't be!" Katch snapped.

"Hush, Katch," Aliena said, laying a hand on his shoulder. "There are many things we don't know about our world." Arthur and Modred exchanged a look agreeing in silence.

Padraig stepped forward politely, smiling at everyone. "The Enchantment touches your world at certain points through portals. Something, or someone, on the RealWorld side, has come close to throwing open these portals. This naturally concerns us."

Yaustis fluttered again. "Because if that happens, the powerful magicks of the Enchantment will be prey to whoever is trying to open the portals." He looked down at Aliena. "Could it be Karayahn and these techno-wizards?"

Aliena shrugged, but it was not a casual motion. "It could be," she admitted. "We don't know the extent of their power. I've heard that her power devices are dimming, even the magical lights in her stronghold. A flying spy device of hers that was following me just sputtered out and fell from the sky. We commonfolk use candles, torches and oil lamps for light and we steal whatever techno-wizard weapons we can." She indicated the laser knives at her wrists. "Otherwise, it is swords, bows and arrows, clubs and the like."

A silence descended as everyone contemplated the significance of this. Modred leaned close to Arthur and whispered, "Great, so you and I are commonfolk. What in hell are techno-wizards?"

"We'll have to find out," Arthur whispered back. "I doubt even Merlin knows." Then he straightened his shoulders and moved toward Aliena. "I'll tell you what, little songsayer, I will offer the resistance my expertise as an old soldier. If you know where I can do that...?"

Aliena shifted on her feet and appeared to think about her answer. Should she trust this strong stranger? He did come to her aid earlier. "Uh... I'm told the resistance base might be found in the city of Tinabulon. All the caravan routes lead to it."

Arthur looked toward Merlin significantly, his mind already made up. "All right then. At dawn's light, to Tinabulon. Where... I hope... there will be ample time for many questions...and answers."

Merlin nodded briefly. Others in the group glanced around and wondered what would really happen next. And if any helpful answers really existed.

Chapter 8

"Answers! I want answers! Now!" Karayahn's voice echoed through the stronghold, bouncing off the corridor walls as she strode through a long passage. Her green, flowing robes were heavy and she had a habit of holding them up to keep them clean. God forbid they drag the floor of her stronghold. She had people to do the sweeping after all. Her black hair with only a few touches of gray, was upswept into a metal crown. Tryon, the tall, thin techno-wizard who accompanied her, cringed as she shouted her way into a large laboratory chamber where slaves worked, attending power generators. "Why is the power failing?" Karayahn demanded.

Tryon caught the door the tall stately woman had slammed open and shut it firmly. Grand Magician Lycenia Karayahn always demanded answers and was never patient in waiting for them. At 55, she was still quite attractive and would have been more so had it not been for the deep frown lines on her forehead and the downward pull that her greed and negativity had created on her mouth. Tyron bowed to her, an obedient techno-wizard paying courtesy to his Grand Magician when he really hungered for even a smidge of her controlling power. He then gestured to indicate the huge machine that dominated the big room. It resembled a cannon but atop it was a massive white crystal embedded in a nest of machinery and wires; the starcystal that only techno-wizards attended.

"Grand Magician, the Aregnans used the starcystal sparingly, and then only for such things as boosting agricultural output in a poor year."

"Fools," Karayahn snapped.

Tryon bowed again, trying to buy favor. "Ah...yes. Since you captured it, however, it's been used to generate all the power in the stronghold." He gestured around widely. "To grow all the fruit and vegetables required by your kitchens... and as a weapon on those occasions when you felt that a demonstration of power..."

Karayahn spun to face him directly and raised her voice again. "Get to it, Tryon!"

Tryon backed away a step, but made it look like he took half a bow. "Yes, Grand Magician. Simply put, all that has been a great drain on the crystal. If it fell from the sky, as the Aregnans said, there is no way to replace it. Certainly, no other has been found."

Karayahn scowled darkly and paced back and forth a few steps. "But what is the life of the crystal? What's the limit?" She fixed a stare on Tryon, demanding an answer.

All he could do was shake his head futilely. "We tried every conceivable way to restore power to it. <u>Nothing</u> worked." He sighed. "When it's drained, it will be the end. The machine can be used for a while to..." He took another deep breath. "...to raise crops. Or for a short period as a supreme weapon. Either way, it is at your disposal. No one can advise you how to use it... unless one advised you not to use it at all. As poor a choice as any." He spread his hands and shrugged; it was all he had to offer.

Karayahn stared at him for a long moment then turned and left the laboratory. Tryon had no alternative but to follow her into the huge, dim corridor outside. A few dark birds fluttered high among the rafters. The Grand Magician ignored them as she moved down the corridor thoughtfully. Tryon walked beside her for several yards before she spoke again.

"Do you know of... the portals?"

Tryon hesitated briefly, then replied, "I've heard of doors... gates into the OtherWorld."

"They exist."

Karayahn stopped and moved to the wall, where a series of small twinkling lights provided the illumination for the corridor. She moved her fingers gently over a series of them, making the pattern change shape and design. "There's great magic on the other side of those portals," she said softly. "Magic to be stolen and utilized in this world. When I studied more of the Aregnan family history, I found repeated references to a hereditary psychokinetic ability. It included knowledge of how to open those doors, but the Aregnans never tampered with the OtherWorld. They had almost been completely exterminated before I realized I needed one alive." She gazed out a window, proud that she was responsible for the murder of a whole ruling dynasty even though it was one with which she had a personal connection.

Tryon ventured carefully, "Lady Greer?"

Karayahn smiled at him wryly. "Shall we visit?" She made a careful gesture at the array of lights on the wall, and they suddenly began to blink in a sequence that activated a large panel beside them. It slid up silently and smoothly, revealing the entrance to a bedchamber. The Grand Magician gestured for Tryon to follow her as she entered.

Inside the well-furnished chamber, a middle-aged woman sat at her dressing table, staring into the small, ancient, but beautiful mirror that faced her. It sat on a small, round base, but could be handheld. The moment she spied the Grand Magician come in, she began to fuss with her hair in a twittering "crazy old lady" way. Her nurse, an older serving woman, glanced up sharply from sewing she held in her hands and turned toward the door.

"Lady Karayahn!"

Karayahn pushed briskly toward the two in the middle of the chamber. "Out of the way, Ona," she snapped.

"Please, Grand Magician," Ona pleaded. "Lady Greer is not well today."

Karayahn stopped two feet away. "What day has she been well? Make her know I am here."

Ona turned back to Greer and began to stroke her arm gently. Her voice went soft and soothing. "My lady, oh, my dearest Greer, can you come to yourself?"

Greer kept primping and playing with her hair, studying herself in the mirror and occasionally making little humming-type noises. Ona stroked her arm again. The... dark mistress, she has come again."

Greer hummed a bit louder.

Karayahn suddenly stormed across to Greer, snarling, "Thrice a week, year in, year out! It is the same charade!" She flung out a hand and knocked over the mirror. The base snapped off the silver handle as it crashed on the dressing table top. Greer started at the sound and stared at the broken mirror, looking like she might burst into tears.

For just an instant, Karayahn's face showed a flash of remorse. "I, I'll have it repaired," she said softly.

Greer nodded sadly and picked up the base. She stroked it gently, as if soothing the broken piece.

"Will we play our same old games, Greer?" Karayahn asked sharply.

"Games?" Greer said, with just a little smile. "Yes. Jolly games." She lapsed into a repetition of the words. "Games. Lames. Tames. Jolly games. Same old ones. Games."

Karayahn sighed and turned to Tryon, who had watched silently. He shook his head. "I didn't know she was simple. The cousin to the Prince Elector...." He shook his head again.

"She went mad watching her family put to the knife," Karayahn said matter of factly. "That's what the nurse says, anyway. I found her so."

"Then why do you keep her?"

"She possesses the power to open the portals into the OtherWorld. Erratic as that is, I want it." Karayahn turned back to Greer, who still bent over the broken mirror, mumbling incoherently. "You know what I want, Greer! Open a portal to let me through, and this nightmare will end."

"Yes," Ona snapped, "she knows you'll kill her."

The Grand Magician turned savagely on the nurse, slapping her to the floor with one heavy blow. Greer cried out and tried to reach toward Ona. Karayahn shoved Greer back hard on her stool and then grabbed the nurse by her thick mass of greying hair, forcing her head back. Greer cried out, holding one hand in a warding-off gesture.

"Yes, you understand now, don't you?" Karayahn sneered. "You understand pain at least, Lady Aregnan." She took a black-bladed knife from a sheath at her belt and put it against Ona's exposed throat. "Then understand this. Open the portal. Open it now! Or I swear I'll roll her head across your foot."

Tryon watched, not liking what his leader was doing, but without the courage to protest. And it <u>might</u> work. Greer could not fight the threat in front of her. Weeping, Greer closed her eyes and concentrated, her fingers lightly touching her temples.

Excited, Karayahn watched as the last Aregnan concentrated. A tiny crystal on the dressing table began to dance and tinkle. Power seemed to crackle around Greer – unseen, tangible power... erratic, weak, but there.

"Go on... open it," Karayahn growled. "Open it!"

Suddenly, Greer let out a gasp. The door of the chamber popped open, and Greer fell limply across the dressing table. Tryon nodded, smiling, impressed.

Karayahn let Ona go and screamed, "Not <u>that</u> door, you dried-up old biddy! Damn you!"

Ona began to struggle to her feet, holding out a pleading hand. "Please, Mistress...."

Karayahn angrily pounded her fists on her own thighs in frustration. "I know she can understand. I know she has the power. Damn it! Damn it to hell!"

Ona moved to Greer and smoothed her hair as Greer wept, sobbing softly. "She's frightened," Ona protested. "So frightened. She can do nothing if she is this afraid. Poor, poor lady."

Beaten, for now, Karayahn straightened, picked up her skirts and marched toward the door. "Enough," she snarled. "Come with me, Tryon, before you hurt yourself laughing."

Tryon wiped the beginning smile from his face and followed. "Yes, Grand Magician," he said, hiding any chuckle that might have escaped. "I believe we both have a few more bugs to iron out of our special... weapons."

They exited, and the door closed, not so smoothly this time but in spurts of power. The Grand Magician kicked it in fury. "Does nothing still work around here?" and she was gone.

For a moment, Greer's shoulders still bounced as if she were crying. Then she raised her head, and Ona could see her laughter, tears running down her cheeks. "Once more, wacky old woman insanity pays off," Greer chuckled. Then she turned her attention to Ona and touched the woman's bruised cheek. "She hurt you."

"It's nothing, my lady." Ona straightened her shoulders and forced a smile.

Greer stood and brushed her hands down her skirt. "It doesn't matter what happens to me," she said curtly. "I don't play the mad woman for myself or even to protect the portals." She turned to gaze out the window, staring into the distance. "My one concern now is keeping the secret from that she-wolf."

"Can you still hope the Aregnan heir lives, my lady?" Ona raised an eyebrow, clearly skeptical.

Greer turned to her, finding a little smile. "We were there when the child was born and smuggled out." She ran a hand over her brow lightly. "Every now and then, I feel... it's like a light touch against my mind... a tickle. As though one of my own has reached out, perhaps in a restless dream." She patted Ona's arm lightly. "Tell you a little secret. I wasn't sure I could, you know? Being only a second cousin." She glanced down at the broken mirror base. "But when I concentrate very hard, I <u>can</u> open the gates."

She waved her hand over the mirror in a distinct, sure movement. The base moved toward the handle and locked on. Greer looked up at Ona. "But as quickly as I do, I lock them up tight again."

The broken mirror's base and handle blended solidly into a clean, hard repair. Ona caught her breath.

"When she returns, she'll see the repair".

Greer nodded and, a bit sadly, used her power to break the handle from the base again.

Chapter 9

As the sun rose over their encampment, Aliena packed up her belongings, noticing Artos putting out the last of their campfire and staring
into the distance. She shaded her eyes against the morning sun's rays to
lock onto his target, a layer of dust on the horizon. Were more assassins
or Garrum guards approaching? "Have they found us?"

Arthur crushed the last of the embers with his foot. "Look closer."

She could now see multiple wagons and pack animals piled high
with trade goods moving their way. "A caravan."

"You said there were many heading to Tinabulon. The assassins and
guards are surely searching for us. Best if we move within greater numbers."

Aliena nodded. "Yes, but these caravan leaders are tough and mer-
cenary. We will have to convince them to take us on."

Artos checked the small purse of gold he carried. It wasn't much.
"This won't do that much convincing."

Suddenly, the songsayer flicked her wrists releasing the spinning
laser knives with which she was so adept in their recent fight. "These
might." A sly smile spread across her face.

Shocked at her sudden action, Arthur jumped back almost a foot
and bumped into a sleepy Katch. He steadied the boy to keep him
from flopping to the ground. Katch nodded to him, acknowledging
the help. Yaustis fluttered awake as Padraig pulled his sword followed
by Tiberius and finally Modred. Tiberius nodded Modred's way. "All

right, slicker! Finally ready, are ya?" Modred glared back as Tiberius looked inquisitively at Aliena. "Uh, what are we ready for?"

She looked into the distance again. "Caravans can always use a few skillful protectors."

Beige and his reunited Foresters were also on the road to Tinabulon, stalking the rich caravan. Done with being a city official in the Grand Magician's realm after enduring the pain of the Garrums' lash on his back, Beige had retreated back into the brotherly comfort of his band of highwaymen.

As the Foresters' horses snaked through crumbling ruins of an old world cathedral, Stellar spurred his mount forward to join his old friend. "So we go for Coloran's outfit yet again. That old mutant must feel us on his heels from miles away by now."

Beige straightened a bit in his saddle and shrugged. "His goods are still rich. Nothing wrong with pulling up to a familiar watering hole".

Stellar could read his leader easily by now. "There are many ways to quench a thirst, old friend. That fiery little songsayer is on the run. I wouldn't mind sampling a bit of her nectar."

Beige reined in his horse and turned, a bit too quickly. "She has nothing to do with this! Nobody signed us on as her protectors. Besides, we don't know that she is headed to Tinabulon."

Stellar smiled. "From what I saw at the Inn, she doesn't need much protection, anyway. Calm down, Connery. Women just complicate things. We keep our eyes on the prize."

Beige guided his horse forward and down a small hill. "Of course. Have I ever done otherwise?" Stellar chuckled under his breath and followed.

As the caravan moved along the trail, Coloran rode at the head of the column. A grizzled, dark mutant, squat, hunched and with a frightening face that was only saved by an odd sense of humor, he used a Belgian draft horse as his mount. The big stallion had been named Chrysalys by the woman who raised him, but Coloran had immediately dubbed him "Chrys." The merchant had been half-sleeping, lulled by the even, steady gait of his horse along the familiar trail; but he snapped awake as Chrys slammed to a stop when Aliena stepped out from behind a large rock in front of him.

"Whoa!" Coloran shouted in alarm. "Who...?" He stared at the girl and the group of men and a boy who followed her...and that big winged...thing.

Aliena smiled pleasantly and held up her hand in greeting. "Coloran. I'm glad it's you." Coloran stared at her, perplexed. "You do remember me, don't you? I traveled with you at least twice before. Aliena... songsayer?"

"Ah... yes. But why...?" Coloran cocked an eyebrow at her and her escorts.

Aliena pointed to the caravan behind him. "We need a ride to Tinabulon. We can't pay." Aliena shrugged. "But we can protect you, should anything, or anyone threaten you." She casually waved toward her companions.

Arthur, Modred, Padraig and Tiberius all slid their swords slightly out of their sheaths, as though choreographed. Yaustis fluttered his wings and tried to look menacing. Katch stood next to Yaustis, almost hidden by the huge creature. Aliena lifted her free arm and triggered the whirling laser knife blade at her wrist. She shut it off and looked questioningly at Coloran.

"Ah..." Coloran hesitated and then shrugged. "Why not?" He assumed that the songsayer and her cohorts were on the run or why would they want to travel with him but he was short on guards on this particular run so he waved at the train of wagons behind him. "Pick a place to ride. I trust you'll be on the lookout for any trouble that might come up."

Aliena smiled brightly. "You have it." She waved to the others. "You heard him. Pick a wagon."

As they moved toward a nearby wagon, Modred glanced at Arthur. "That went well. Girl's a real talker."

"And she has those glowing knives on her wrists," Arthur said, smiling. This little songsayer continued to grow on him. Quite a woman; smart, talented and battle-ready. He felt something stirring in him that had slept for impossible eons. He both liked and was wary of it.

By moonrise, Aliena, Arthur and company, accepted as guards and scouts for Coloran's caravan, had traveled deep into the Outlands, passing broken remnants of skeletal skyscrapers and crumbling roads once traveled by machines rumored in legend to move far faster than the horses and beasts of burden pushing and pulling the caravan forward. Arthur and Merlin sat on the back of a wobbly wagon. Arthur turned to his old wizardly teacher with a puzzled look on his face. "So many things I don't understand, Merlin. You must have at least some of the answers."

"Not as many as you may think. But ask as you choose. I'll try to help you."

Arthur frowned, took a deep breath and began hesitantly. "We are still in Britain?"

"Yes but it is called Gritania now."

Arthur considered this. "Very well but that cave I awoke in...those large glass boxes that...hummed and...sang..."

"Yes," Merlin nodded. "Not of the world you knew. Or mine, either. The beings who came to me were human in appearance, but they had a strangeness. However, I felt somehow...safe with them. Now that I've met Padraig, I think they must have been his people...from the Enchantment. They told me it was prophesized that you were the king who would not die...that there was a future when you would return to serve…and save England when she needed you most. They promised to preserve you with their 'ways", as they put it."

"That cave and those boxes."

Merlin smiled thinly. "Indeed but first we did give your body a most worthy funeral."

"Oh?"

"Oh, yes. Three weeping queens escorted you on a boat to an island in a great lake. Your subjects offered prayers as your body sailed out of sight."

"I awoke in a cave in a hillside far from any…great lake."

"Yes. Your body was moved there by those strangers. They promised I would live to see you arise in this…our future. And I have lived through so much I cannot tell you all that has happened."

The wagon hit a rock and lurched. Arthur and Merlin had to restack a few overturned containers before returning to their conversation. Arthur struggled to express the many questions that had plagued him since arriving. "This land is full of inventions that are far beyond our understanding, especially weapons that don't seem to be from the time of those who carry them. The villages, the system now is similar to our time but…" Arthur looked into the distance where tall, boxy buildings lay in ruin. "Almost nothing remains of their structures". He looked at the strange moon with its circling debris field. "And the moon…was there a great war?"

Merlin nodded. "I slept, part of the time, in my own magical trance until I was needed. But yes, their legends say it started in a land across the great sea where brother turned on brother and split the realm in two. As in your time, trust was rare and betrayal and greed prevailed. There were two philosophies and no compromise, no tolerance. The beliefs spread world-wide. No man could be neutral. Power-mad rulers replaced republics in which ordinary people had a say. They had great technology and almost destroyed humanity. What we are living in now is the result; common man scrabbling to survive under a ruler with no empathy determined to control what remains of Man's technology while the unenlightened call it "magic".

Arthur bowed his head. What could he, one man, do to change anything? Would humankind forever repeat its horrible errors? He would change the sad subject. "How did you know where I was?"

"I didn't." Merlin smiled. "I made them promise they would include something in the cave and with the clothing you would find." He pointed at Arthur's belt with its unique buckle.

"It's magic...like yours."

"My magic," Merlin replied nodding. "I took a bit of my blood and made it part of your buckle. I did the same with your blood and my buckle. I've worn mine for centuries, waiting for it to awaken. When it did, I knew you were alive, and it would lead me to you."

"At the Outlands Inn." Arthur smiled ruefully. "When I needed to be rescued."

"All our new friends needed to be...at least aided, if not rescued."

Arthur rested his hand on his sword hilt. "We didn't do too badly, even if your rainstorm did boost our exit." He patted the hilt again. "At least you have not changed," he chuckled. "That was quite the storm."

Merlin frowned as a brief sorrow moved over him. "No, I'm a deceiver now, too. My powers have faded as I've aged, and I could only create that magic in an enclosed space." He shook his head. "Outside...my magic is weaker." Arthur placed a hand on his shoulder in support. Changing the subject slightly, he asked, "Why wasn't Excalibur in the cave?"

Merlin sighed. "That I can't answer. When you fell on the field, apparently dead, a great hand came out of the sky, lifted Excalibur and drew it into the clouds. Many people felt that your heart and soul went with it."

"Perhaps it did," Arthur said quietly. He glanced up at the red-ringed moon. "Perhaps it did."

Arthur looked around to see Modred, who rode nearby. Modred caught the look and pointedly looked away.

"So now is when I'm needed most? And what about him? Why was Modred placed with me? And of all my good and worthy knights, why was he the only one to survive?"

Merlin frowned in puzzlement. "I simply do not know." Merlin's eyes went to Modred who didn't see this but he touched his sword restlessly, as if feeling the wizard's stare. "The beings who placed you in the cave may not have predicted this outcome."

Leaning in closer to Merlin, Arthur near whispered, "Should I trust him? He is ever the betrayer but here and now, we are all strangers in this strange land. We need one another."

"Trust only the dark instincts in him. His ears can hear shadows, and his eyes pick out daggers beneath cloaks. Modred is...Modred."

As if overhearing, Modred snatched his hood back; and his sword was in his hand. His eyes searched the desert under the reddish moonlight. Arthur hopped off the back of the cart to come to the side of Modred's mount.

"Something?"

Modred leaned down to speak to his king in a whisper. "Count! There are more riders in the caravan than when we joined it."

Aliena suddenly rode up from a distance to join them, bringing Arthur's horse. "We may have to earn our keep as guards for this ragtag outfit. Something isn't right." Modred turned to face her. Could she read his mind?

Chapter 10

Inside Karayahn's fortress, Lady Greer toyed with her treasured, broken mirror. Suddenly, she took in a startled breath. Her devoted servant, Ona, was instantly at her side. "What is wrong, my lady?"

"That was more than a tickle. I'm more sure now than ever. The Aregnan heir is out there, and he or she is in danger and on high alert." She turned and took Ona's hand. "But there is hope, Ona. I not only felt a bit of apprehension, but a great strength and determination. I don't think the child knows it yet, but the heir is far more powerful than we ever dreamed."

Ona took a deep breath and caressed Lady Greer's hand. "Let us hope, my lady. Let us hope."

In another part of the caravan, Coloran had been riding half-asleep in his saddle, but woke to find a sword at his throat. He was surprised, but knew better than to make a hasty move. "Ohhhhh. Don't tell me."

Beige threw back his hood and stood up in his stirrups. "You must admit, I'm pretty good." Then, yelling, "In fact, we're all pretty good. What say you, Foresters?"

Stellar Blue, Wolfer, Aaron, Jobair and Jorn revealed themselves and shouted a hearty chorus of "We're great!" "Aye! Foresters forever!" as they trained their weapons on Coloran and his drivers and the caravan came to a slow halt. A hooded Aliena had split off from Arthur and Modred and sat calmly on her horse nearby. She had turned Katch over to Tiberius. The boy was overly anxious to help and had pulled a small knife from his boot. The elf grabbed the reins of Katch's horse and pulled him close. "Put that away, ya little welp!" Katch frowned but complied.

Coloran easily recognized his old nemesis. "Might'a known many crossings without being robbed was too much to expect." Beige hopped up on a wagon and bowed to the members of the caravan. He raised his voice. "On this rare night, you have the even more rare privilege of being held up by Connery Beige and his Foresters of the Moon."

"And to what do we owe this 'rare privilege,' Marshal Beige?" Aliena said strongly and mockingly. Beige was bowled over by the sound of her voice. She pulled back her hood, got off her mount and grinned up at him.

His mouth dropped open. "You? It is! Gods, woman, I thought you were dead by now." He offered a hand and pulled her up onto the wagon beside him.

"I thought the same for a time, Marshal."

"Oh, it's just Beige now. No more Manor House or occupation guards for me. Back to the banditry, the sword and the bow!"

Wolfer and Stellar exchanged an eye-rolling glance. "Uh, speaking of banditry," Wolfer asked bluntly, "are we going to get on with it or what?"

Beige shot a "back off" stare at Wolfer. "Just hold on a while."

Aliena and Beige continued their conversation as if a hold-up wasn't in progress. She turned to him. "But why? Why leave a safe situation?"

Beige lifted up his shirt and turned, showing her his back. She winced as she looked at the ugly scars. "A taste of the Dragon's Tongue convinced me to...uh...resign my exalted post."

Still ribbing his old cohort, Stellar moved a bit closer to Aliena. "He heard the Garrum officer sending the assassins after you and took your part. Surely that deserves a kiss or two?" The Foresters laughed, as did a few of the Caravaners.

Aliena met Beige's eyes. "Oh really?"

"Seems my men always know the best rewards are seldom weighed in gold." He pulled her closer and put an arm around her waist.

She backed him off with an icy stare. "Those rewards aren't passed out to highwaymen."

Taking a step back, Beige continued the "game." "And just who are they passed out to?"

Frowning, she fired back, "Only to the enemies of Karayahn."

Pulling Aliena close again, Beige smiled down at her. "Well then pucker up, my sweet lass." She pushed him away more strongly this time.

Wolfer had had enough of this flirty game. "Connery, are we going to rob this caravan or not?"

"Yes, what says the bandit leader?" snapped Aliena sharply as she hopped off the back of the wagon and spun the laser knives at her wrists.

Arthur, Merlin, Tiberius and Modred, who had been keeping their distance, moved a bit closer with hands on weapons. Caravan boss Coloran watched the proceedings with impatience and finally shouted to Aliena, "I let you and your lot join my outfit to protect it. Well...start protecting!"

Beige sighed and made his decision. "Oh well, obviously we're going to let this one go. It's a pretty poor one anyway." Coloran sniffed, offended...but not too obviously. He wouldn't want Beige to change his mind.

As the Foresters grumbled, Wolfer turned to Jorn. "Looks like we are not going to get rich if the caravans start carrying pretty women with them."

Jorn smiled and launched a wide grin at Wolfer. "But I might become a caravan driver."

Beige got off the wagon. Aliena touched his arm and, in a bit more kindly tone, said, "Come with us to Tinabulon."

"Tinabulon? Aliena, Tinabulon's teaming with thieves and cut-throats of every sort. My Foresters would be lost in the crowd there. We need to spread our skills to the far corners of the realm where robbers are a rare lot."

She glanced around and moved a bit closer and, in almost a whisper, she said, "There is going to be a rebellion against Karayahn, and we can use men like you."

That made him pause for the smallest of instants before he shrugged off her plea. "Rebels? Sorry, I've no taste for anything else the Garrum have to pass out to Marshals, thieves or...gods deliver us...rebels."

Aliena turned, remounted her horse and then sniped back. "All right, go on! Go rob caravans, brawl in bars, drink and whore and revel in being a damn outlaw legend." The Foresters nodded their heads in affirmation...sounded good to them. She moved her mount closer and looked Beige directly in the eyes. "Just remember this, Connery Beige. Fate has given you a second chance. You were a legend once, and now you've gotten a chance to be one again...only not as a thief. Shuck it off if you want but if fate tries to deal you in a second time, you better think twice before you pass. You can help lead what's left of the world back to a place in the sun or lie in your grave forgotten...forever!"

Arthur, who had been sitting on his horse off to the side watching the exchange between the songsayer and the highwayman, suddenly snapped his attention to what Aliena had just said. The words echoed in his mind. "Help lead the world back...or lie in your grave forgotten." Hadn't she just struck the exact reason he was here? Why had he been brought back to life now, in this place if this was not the reason?

A much more solemn Beige looked at his Foresters, who were also at attention after such a speech. Aliena moved her horse forward. "Get this train moving, Coloran. It's a long way to Tinabulon." Arthur moved up to ride beside her. He had just developed a new respect and perhaps more for this brave and determined woman.

Left behind, Beige was lost in thought. The caravan moved past the Foresters, and Beige looked around at his band. They wouldn't look at one another...or him. Aliena's sharp words had definitely registered. Did he feel more for this woman than a dallying interest? Her songs had always charmed him but...it was more. He had to admit it. He sighed and spurred away, riding off at a right angle from the departing caravan. The Foresters followed glumly. ****

As the lights of the caravan moved into the distance, Beige and his men reached the top of a sandy hill, watching their would-be mark getting away. Beige was still making a decision. "What, uh, what did she say about my grave?"

Wolfer pulled his mount closer. "Forgotten."

Stellar pulled up on the other side. "Forever."

"That's what I thought she said." Suddenly, Beige urged his horse forward down the sandy hill.

"Where are you going?" shouted a confused Jobie, who stared as Beige continued down the hill riding toward the caravan.

"I suddenly realized how much I want to see good old Tinabulon again!" Beige shouted back over his shoulder.

Jobie grinned at the others and kicked his horse to follow his leader. "I hope glory makes a warm shroud."

"Wonder what stupidity makes?" asked Wolfer, following behind them as well as Stellar.

"Wolfer, the only difference between a rut and a grave is the depth!"

And the Foresters rode again, united in a new cause.

Chapter 11

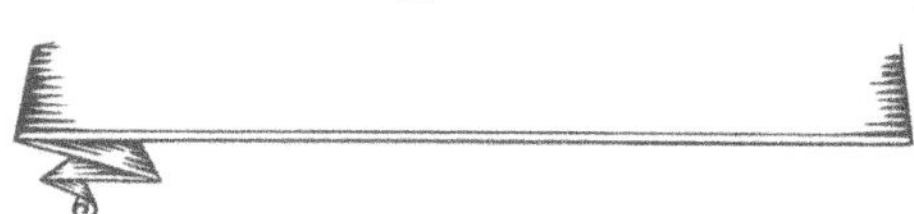

The Outlands sun now glared down on the caravan as a disappointed Aliena rode at the head. If only Beige and his men would have agreed to join the rebels. Maybe she misjudged him. Despite an attraction for any "bad boy", she knew there had always been an electricity between them. But, he'd always be out for himself. Arthur pulled his horse up beside her, just as they were passing the crumbled ruins of a huge citadel that, most likely, didn't exist in his time.

"You handled yourself quite well back there," Arthur offered.

"I've ridden the caravan roads before. One learns to think and talk fast."

"No. What you said to Connery Beige and his men, you spoke like a recruiting general to a band of cutthroats who could easily have killed you."

"It fell on deaf ears, and I'm no general but..." She locked eyes with him. "I could use one."

"Just how deeply are you involved in this revolt?"

She paused. How much should she tell him? Was he as trustworthy as she suspected or just a very good actor? "I've devoted my life to it, but we aren't nearly ready and it worries me."

The caravan pulled to the side of the road to water the horses. Aliena and Arthur dismounted, leading their mounts to water barrels hitched to the side of one wagon. As the horses drank, she leaned against the wagon. "And you, where do you come from and why offer to help? You never give me a straight answer."

She had trusted him but Arthur knew he mustn't say too much. "I understand your cause. As I told you, I am a soldier. I suppose I've always fought because I believe in justice, in peace. I won them once, but they are difficult to hold." His eyes seemed fixed as his mind flew back briefly to his knights, the table, the old realm he once ruled. Aliena could feel his pain and moved a bit closer to him. "We're a raw force, Artos. So far, we've only managed to annoy Karayahn's men. We have to do more. We have to fight as a unit." She was pleading. "Can you help us? Train our people? Help lead them?"

He smiled. He knew this was coming. It was evidently his fate. "Dear lady, I am at your service." He bowed to her.

"And I." The voice came from behind the wagon. Beige and his men had caught up. He had overheard the exchange between Artos and Aliena and was not pleased. It was more evident than ever that he admired the songsayer's beauty and spunk himself.

Aliena scanned the area, sighting the rest of the Forester band. "So you're with us then?" Beige nodded as she and Arthur re-mounted. She kicked her horse forward. "Then we move on. It's another day to Tinabulon". Beige guided his horse a little too quickly in front of Arthur to ride at her side. Arthur was both amused and a little miffed. He shrugged, found a small smile and reined in behind them.

Night had again fallen on the Outlands. The caravan was camped at the base of tumbled, once multi-storied ruins that offered shelter from wind and weather. Merlin and Katch sat close together beside a campfire. More fires flickered nearby. At one, Aliena sat alone, strumming her lyrit. Beige and his men huddled around another while Arthur and Modred, as well as the group from the Enchantment, busily lit their own.

Merlin held a short, sharp dagger which he showed Katch. He held it toward the firelight and it glistened with menace. Merlin palmed it and deftly produced a delicate rose in its place. The boy's eyes grew wide.

"You see, boy, what appears to be an object of destruction can often be converted to a thing of beauty and peace."

Katch's eyes grew even wider. "How did you do that?"

Merlin smiled. "Simple magic, sleight of hand."

"Oh, let me try!" Merlin handed him the dagger. Katch tried once and failed. Then, he palmed the dagger successfully. Proud of himself, the boy smiled; but his grin turned to a frown when he realized something missing. "But, where do I get the rose?"

Merlin laughed, perhaps remembering another boy and similar questions. "Ha! That, my boy, is the true magic."

Aliena, who had moved nearby carrying her lyrit. joined them. Artos came from another direction. She sat down. "It'll take more than simple tricks to stop Karayahn."

"The monsters say they are powerful enough to scare her at least," said Katch.

"Monsters?" Arthur inquired, sitting next to Aliena.

"Yaustis and his friends, Padraig and Tiberius", Katch explained.

Aliena frowned and wiped dirt from her young brother's forehead. "You know they don't like you calling them that."

Katch never liked to be scolded by his sister. He frowned and moved a little away from her but she continued. "They're gentlefolk from an ancient and glorious land of crystal towers and strong magic." Katch stared at the fire, and it suddenly flared.

"Padraig told me there is incredible power inside their gates", the boy related. "Such as they have crossed our path before and told of many wonders." Katch looked into the near distance at the Enchantment band sitting around their own fire.

Aliena picked up the story. "Their Council has sent them here. You mustn't forget that their world is threatened, too. That's why they've joined us. Karayahn's thirst for power is insatiable, and she's made them her next mark."

Behind a ruined wall, Modred, hunched low, snuck through tumbled ruins until he spotted Yaustis, Padraig and Tiberius at their campfire. The thween looked on as his cohorts spoke in serious tones. Modred moved closer and hunkered down behind the wall to listen, unobserved.

"We were sent to find out for sure who is knockin' on our doors", said Tiberius as he paced back and forth, glowering at his companions.

"If these humans can help us..." began Padraig.

"Then we need to join them," Yaustis said flatly, with a flutter of his wings.

Tiberius kicked a stone angrily. "I don't join up with any critter who takes one look and calls me a monster!"

Yaustis tried reason. "We've not spent a lot of time on this side of the gates, Tiberius. If Karayahn is our enemy, we need to join the humans to combat her." Tiberius accelerated his agitated pacing, hands clasped behind his back. Yaustis fluttered closer, trying for logic. "I think Padraig should go back to the Council and inform them of the situation." His ears tweaked and fluttered. "There is another portal some way ahead of us, near our destination."

Modred moved even closer. He was more than interested as, from his carry bag, Tiberius produced the plett. Modred's interest sharpened even more at the sight of the round object.

"Here's the plett then," said Tiberius. "You're it, Paddy." He held the object out to Padraig, who threw up his hands in defeat as he accepted the key.

"All right. I'll go back when we reach Tinabulon."

Always looking for knowledge that could advance his fortune even in this bizarre new world, Modred smiled in satisfaction. Now he could get his hands on future bargaining power.

Very late that night, Merlin and Katch had curled up in make-shift bedrolls, asleep. Aliena sat quietly, her fingers lightly stroking the strings of her lyrit. She seemed to be working out a tune in her head. Arthur leaned in closer. "That is beautiful."

She smiled. "I was just listening to an old song in my head."

He was curious. "That harp…"

"Lyrit."

"I have never seen anything like it. Where…I come from, we have harps. Something like that, but usually larger. Not so easy to hold and carry."

There it was again "Where I come from". Was he ever going to share his true origin with her? Aliena nodded. "I've heard of things such as you describe. But long ago in our land. The lyrit came about as an instrument that could be carried even into battle, if need be." She stroked the strings again lightly, producing a sweet chord that seemed to quiver in the air. "We've needed battle songs in the past."

Arthur smiled, enjoying the conversation. "Where did this instrument come from? A family heirloom?"

"Ah, sort of." Aliena's grin went wide, and she hugged the lyrit closer. "I'm told that my grandfather made it for me when I was a baby and said he knew I would learn to play it as I grew. He said it would be part of me all my life and it has been."

Arthur tilted his head, curious. "How did he know you would be…so musical? Others in your family?"

"No. No one. I never knew him but I think…maybe his father or mother sang. He told my parents that I would be master of the lyrit. And I became a songsayer because of that. It just seemed…right."

Arthur smiled, remembering what he'd heard her sing. "'A Star to Steer By'. It carries a most inspiring message. You would have been well received…uh…in my country."

It was as if he were teasing her, playing some kind of guessing game. It was maddening. "You're never going to tell me where you come from, are you?" She crooked an eyebrow, perhaps a challenge. "If you're a wanted man, join the club. You should know that you can trust me."

He drew a deep breath. She wasn't going to let this go. How would he answer? "It's a place far from here. A different kind of world and life. And yet...not so very different in some ways."

"What ways?"

He considered a long moment, then smiled at her. "You ask a difficult question. But one thing I can say is that life is hard for all of us. Everywhere. The world needs strong and fair leadership, and the people should have a safe and peaceful life to live, one in which they have a say."

She gave up her quest to know more about this intriguing mystery man...for now. At least his beliefs matched hers. "You fit in very well with our resistance."

"Yes, I do." Arthur took her hand in his, bent over it and kissed it. "I do."

"Oh," she breathed. "Oh." She looked away quickly, hoping he hadn't noticed the leap in her pulse rate when his lips brushed her hand.

Chapter 12

The next morning, the caravan pulled into Tinabulon, a large, true wasteland outpost with all the corruption and respite for weary travelers that entails. Aliena, Arthur and Beige guided their horses to a trading post while the Foresters, Modred and other caravan travelers started to wander the area, looking for a tavern. Locals stared at Yaustis, again blaming his existence on the Grand Magician's experiments and soon ignored him. He and his Enchantment friends stepped aside to talk quietly. Modred, pretending to check his saddle and gear, stood nearby, listening.

Coloran waved the trade wagons ahead to an open area where buyers clustered, waiting eagerly for the new goods to arrive. He thanked the protectors he'd hired while dropping a purse into Aliena's hand. "Do you want to count it?"

She balanced the purse, feeling its weight. "I'll trust you this time...although I shouldn't but I know where you go to ground between trips". Coloran frowned and grumbled as he rode away.

Aliena turned to Beige and Arthur, noticing how bandit Beige was eyeing the purse. She quietly confided, "This goes into our war chest."

"Of course", Beige responded, shrugging his shoulders.

Aliena dismounted and let her horse drink from a trough in front of the weathered trading post. Arthur and Beige did the same. "I know the couple who own this post.

They are friends of mine and they should have news for us."

Beige seemed anxious and impatient. "The only news I'm interested in is how soon we can get some more fighters together and do some damage to Karayahn. Then I can get back to <u>my</u> business."

"Of course". Aliena placed a calming if condescending hand on Beige's arm and Arthur didn't fail to notice that the outlaw warmed at her touch. As the trio walked toward the trading post, Arthur clapped a hand on Beige's back, not knowing of his recent injuries. Beige winced. "We'll be in the thick of things soon enough, my friend." Beige shook off Arthur's hand. "I'm not your friend." Arthur shrugged. This wasn't going to be easy.

Katch ran up to join his sister as the group entered the trading post, the only major supply depot for the large Outland area. Everything from food stuff, dry goods, clothes, both pawned and new jewelry, old, used and newer weapons packed the shelves. Katch ran straight to stare at an assortment of blasters while Xander and Fleya, a kindly middle-aged couple, greeted Aliena.

After scanning the store for any enemies, Aliena relaxed. "Xander, it's fine to see you. Have you good news for us? Do our numbers grow?"

Xander glanced warily at Arthur and Beige. "You can trust them," Aliena assured him. "They've joined us."

Xander bowed in welcome and guided the group to a table and chairs in the back of the store where any unfriendly ears could not overhear. Frowning, he shook his head. "The word ain't good. There are a few still dedicated to freedom at any cost, but most of the crofters and merchants are afraid."

"They could lose everything in a rebellion," said Fleya. Was she speaking for herself as well? "They'd rather stay safe and alive."

Aliena snapped back with a dose of reality. "And feel the wrath of Karayahn's starcrystal if they don't obey her?"

Arthur was puzzled. "Starcrystal?"

Beige all but rolled his eyes. "Where have you been, man? The Crystal is an incredible machine, and Karayahn uses it as a weapon. I've seen it at work. It can reduce a whole settlement to rubble in seconds." Katch approached nearby and overheard Beige continue. "...And what it does to human flesh..." Katch swallowed hard.

Arthur was again befuddled, impressed and appalled with this strange land and time in which he had awakened. "If it has such power, we must gather more than ordinary farmers and merchants to combat it."

Beige, as usual, was convinced his Foresters and others of like mind could be victorious against all odds. "My men will be a match for a battalion of Karayahn's Garrum. If we need more fighters, I'll get them! My name still carries some weight around here...in certain circles, you understand."

Xander and Fleya smiled. This man's enthusiasm was rare and welcome.

Arthur wasn't sure about these "certain circles," but was glad of the possibility. "Good. The more experienced recruits we have, the better our chances. I will go with you."

Beige's eyes flashed angrily at Arthur's suggestion, but Aliena interrupted before he could voice any objection. "I'd go myself, but the Garrum are looking for me. I'll help Fleya prepare our lodgings for the night." She stood up, dismissing the two men who reluctantly teamed up and headed for the door.

On the edge of Tinabulon, the uneasy duo walked through the ruins and rubble of buildings twenty-first century denizens might recognize. To Arthur, all was strange and other-worldly. Beige stopped and picked up a piece of masonry. "There was a tavern here only a few years ago."

Arthur examined the piece of rubble in Beige's hand. "Someone appears to have objected to it."

"The burn marks are from Garrum weapons. They must have just blown the place up, along with the unsavory clientele." Beige's sadness was palpable.

"Friends of yours?"

"Some of them, I imagine."

Arthur looked to the horizon. "And these are the same hellhounds after Aliena."

"Yes. The very same". Beige tossed the piece of masonry aside and walked to a very large nearby drainpipe, an obvious relic of the pre-holocaust.

Arthur joined him, and they leaned against the pipe. "Then we might have more luck looking elsewhere for our army." Beige nodded his agreement. Suddenly, Arthur looked toward a distant hill and straightened to attention. Beige followed his gaze and stiffened as well.

Approaching and coming closer was the biggest, meanest-looking brute one could hope to avoid. He carried a huge longbow, wore leathers and had a laser-scarred face. He was humming his own bawdy pub song to himself. Beige and Arthur reacted to the approach of this hulk with a certain amount of anxiety. Beige slowly donned his laser gauntlet, and Arthur's hand came to rest on his sword hilt.

Beige smiled. "That's a likely lad if ever I saw one."

Arthur was less enthusiastic. "Likely to skewer us with an arrow from that longbow."

Both men concentrated on the man nearing them. Suddenly, a young-looking, wiry, four foot six inch fighter in his mid-30's screeched a horrific battle cry "Aieeeeeeee!!" and jumped out from inside the pipe to a position in front of them. He was dressed in a post-holocaust version of Samurai gear and he seemed to come from nowhere.

Startled beyond belief, Arthur and Beige dove behind the pipe for cover, weapons drawn and ready. The little man drew back the string of a shorter longbow, aimed and let fly. The approaching brute took the arrow in his chest, not knowing what hit him. He fell flat with a loud thud. Beige and Arthur still squatted behind the pipe, taking all of this in. They looked at one another open-mouthed. The little man re-slung his bow over his shoulder and gathered up a small bag of belongings from inside the pipe. Arthur and Beige rose from their hiding spot and approached the mini-warrior, their weapons at rest, but handy. The tiny fighter turned toward them and...bowed. What? They bowed in return.

"That was quite a shot," said Beige with admiration.

"I gather the brigand wasn't in your favor," Arthur ventured.

"He made me lose face," replied the warrior matter-of-factly. He bowed again. "Shang-Sui at your service."

Arthur stepped forward, warily. "Uh, Shang, how would you like to join us on an honorable mission?"

Shang looked doubtful. "I pick my missions in life very carefully. Who's the target?"

Beige moved forward and stated flatly, "Grand Magician Karayahn and her techno-wizards."

Shang smiled very slowly. "You're crazy. But then, that mad cow has made us all lose face. I'm with you!" The three warriors engaged in some friendly back-slapping and handshakes.

Inside the trading post living quarters, Aliena, Merlin and Katch sat on floor cushions, having just finished dinner. Aliena softly played a tune on her lyrit while Merlin watched Katch. He saw a lot of Arthur at that age in the boy. A large goblet was prominent on the floor between them. Katch frowned and stared at the goblet with great concentration. Nothing happened.

Frustrated, he snapped at Merlin. "I don't see why making an old goblet disappear could help us fight the techno-wizards."

Aliena stopped playing to smile at her brother's impatience. Merlin was used to this youthful frustration. "The same skill may be used on other...utensils. Watch." He faced the wall where Xander's blaster hung.

Frowning slightly, he directed a fierce look at it. The blaster began to shimmer, then fade, until it totally disappeared.

Aliena and Katch reacted in awe. Katch was especially excited. "I get it. Poof! No blaster. But, uh, Xander isn't going to be pleased with you. That was his favorite weapon."

"It will soon be with us again." The blaster began to re-materialize. "The effect can be temporary," Merlin said as the blaster fully reformed on the wall. "Try again, Katch."

Katch gazed at the goblet while his hand snuck behind his back with crossed fingers. The goblet flickered and began to fade, only a tiny bit, but enough to see. Then, it solidified again. Disappointed in himself, Katch looked at Merlin. "Maybe if I knew where the power comes from?"

"From within, my boy. Some of us have a gift. I see it in you." He looked at Aliena. "You have it, too, child; but, in you, it is different." Aliena appeared to be very far away, not really hearing. Merlin frowned. He wanted her to hear him. It was important.

Chapter 13

In an alleyway in a different part of Tinabulon, Arthur, Beige and Shang-Sui walked warily.

"There is another tavern in town where I spent a good deal of my youth with...a certain lady." Beige smiled at the memory while a frustrated Arthur stopped, grabbing Beige's arm.

"We hardly have time to visit your ladies."

Beige yanked his arm away. "This lady saved my life, and she's a hellion with a rocket-dagger. We can use her."

Shang sensed the tension between his new comrades and stepped back, watching for Garrum while what had been brewing between the two men came to a boil. Beige planted his feet firmly to face Arthur. "And don't tell me to stay away from women, Duke. I've seen you making eyes at our little general."

Arthur shook his head and turned away. "Your eyes deceive you, Beige."

Beige snorted a brief laugh. "I don't think so."

Music and bawdy laughter from the tavern filled the air as a band of drunks, arm-in-arm, stumbled out and into the alley breaking the tension...for the moment. Beige, Arthur and Shang entered the establishment with Arthur and Beige nodding to Foresters Stellar, Wolfer and Jorn who had, indeed, finally found the town tavern. Several Garrum Guardsmen were at the drinking and gaming tables with other customers, various mutants, traders, gunslinger types and bar girls.

An attractive dark-haired woman in her mid-twenties stood with her back to the entrance. She wore a leather blouse with long, tight-laced sleeves, boots and a neo-Gypsy style skirt. Her name was Harper. On the far wall was a target with a group of diamond shapes, narrowing to a tiny, central diamond. Already stuck in the bullseye were several rocket-daggers. The crowd cheered and jeered at Harper as she prepared her last dagger. They started betting fast and furiously on the outcome.

Harper frowned in concentration as her hand whipped up the last dagger, aimed and released it. The dagger, under rocket power, smashed into the center diamond. The crowd cheered or moaned, depending on how their bets went. Harper smiled and picked up several coins thrown to her. Beige, Arthur and Shang lurked in the shadows, watching the action. Jorn, Wolfer and Stellar, not knowing what Beige, Arthur and their short new companion had planned, kept their distance but paid extra attention to the woman with the daggers. Wolfer frowned. "She looks familiar. Am I right?" Jorn nodded in the affirmative "Yes but can't place her."

Two Garrum Guards entered with a very young female captive, perhaps still in her teenaged years. Her hands were tied but she kept trying to kick the Garrum. Her dirty blonde hair had been unevenly cropped short, her pants were full of holes and a once attractive blue blouse was ripped. Her short hair made it easy to see that the top of her ears appeared to be scalloped, perhaps the result of a few post-holocaust mutant genes. Harper, crossing to retrieve her daggers from the target, watched, concerned as the Garrum dragged the girl to the target and strapped her hands to it. The tavern owner, Thorn, a big-bellied man, pushed forward to face the Garrum. "What's going on?"

The lead guard responded. "She killed three of the Grand Magician's Guardsmen." The crowd booed as they were expected to but half-heartedly. "They killed my father", said the young woman in heart-felt anguish. The crowd laughed while the lead guard turned to Harper.

"Prepare your daggers and move to the far wall. We will make it more of a challenge for your talent."

As the bloodthirsty crowd cheered in approval and bets went down for this new "game," Harper stared at the Garrum with pure hatred. The guards stared back at her in challenge and raised their weapons.

"You pigs. She's only a child!"

The Garrum obviously couldn't care less. "And a killer. Prepare your daggers!"

With no choice, Harper slowly moved toward the back wall as Arthur, Beige and Shang went on alert. Arthur whispered to Beige. "Is that her? The hellion with the daggers?"

"Yes, but this isn't her style. We've got to get her and that girl out of here. Follow my lead." He headed toward the tavern door.

Harper slowly fingered her daggers, taking her time as she loaded the rocket mechanism. She turned toward the target where the girl was strung up. There was a scuffle in the doorway and Beige, now wearing his cloak with the hood up, entered with Arthur. They carried Shang's stiff and apparently dead body while chanting a drunken dirge as they moved forward. The crowd was distracted by this odd procession. Even Harper turned to watch the show as Beige and Arthur laid Shang out on the bar. The Foresters stood at the ready with hands on weapons, should they be needed.

"Drinks here, man. Drinks for our fren," mumbled Beige as Thorn and two of his bouncers approached.

"Get that man off my bar!", yelled Thorn.

Arthur chimed in, "This's our fren' and he be stone dead." "An' we're here ta drink him on his way to the afterworld," added Beige.

"Not in my tavern. Out!" yelled Thorn as he motioned to his bouncers to do their duty.

"Now thass no way ta treat payin' cust'mers," slurred Beige as he threw some coins on the bar, and the bouncers moved in.

Seeing her chance during this interruption, Harper snaked along the wall until she reached the girl and began to untie her. Their eyes met. The girl was afraid. How could this hellion about to skewer her with daggers be a friend? All eyes were on the fracas at the bar where Thorn eyed Shang closely, and the Garrum and customers moved to the bar to get a closer look. Thorn reached out and guardedly poked Shang in the chest, then the cheek. Shang held every muscle rigid. He truly appeared to be dead.

"This little ape is a goner, all right... ugly too," announced Thorn.

Insulted, Shang opened his eyes, jumped up and shrieked his battle cry while half the customers, along with Thorn, nearly jumped out of their skins. In the background, Harper and the girl worked their way toward an exit. Shang grabbed Thorn, and the fight was on with the Foresters joining in.

During the altercation, Harper snapped alert as she recognized Beige when his hood fell back. She used her daggers against the deserving Garrum guard who had strung up the girl. Arthur wielded his sword as only Arthur could. Shang-Sui employed his Samurai fighting skills to great advantage, and the fight escalated to the street.

The raucous crowd exploded out the door, and the girl rushed to a tethered Garrum horse, calmed it with a pat on the nose and drew a weapon from the saddle. It was a powerhead. She rammed it at the back of the Garrum officer who had Arthur pinned down, and it exploded. The officer slumped, dead with a smoking hole in his back. Arthur quickly nodded in appreciation while Thorn took an opportunity to crash a tankard into the face of a guard. Stellar and Jorn quickly incapacitated another Garrum officer. The tide of the battle turned and the travelers managed to escape down an alley and away from the brawl.

While on the run, Harper turned to Beige. "You always manage to turn up at the right moment, but you leave at all the wrong ones."

"You know me so well." He grabbed her hand, which she quickly yanked away.

"That's my misfortune."

Chapter 14

Outside Tinabulon, in a rocky area, the desert stretched away toward the horizon. Padraig approached the base of a craggy cliff and dismounted. A safe distance away, behind the ruin of what must have once been a 21st century office building, Modred dismounted while watching Padraig's every move. Walking to the cliff face, Padraig pulled out the plett and gestured with it, a graceful, mystical move. All the colors of the rainbow flowed from the plett as magic began to unlock the portal. In total awe, Modred watched the wonder unfold.

The cliff face shimmered and disappeared in a myriad of colored lights. The light faded and a fog cleared from the portal opening. One could see into the Enchantment! It was a land of crystal towers; a rich, inviting landscape of streams, rolling green hills; all things bright and beautiful that were so rare in the post holocaust outer world. Padraig stepped through as the fog moved back in. When it cleared, the stone cliff was again solid.

Modred rushed to the cliff, but could only stand with his hands against the cold stone. Everything was as it was before. What was this strong magic? Modred caressed the stone surface and smiled. At least he'd found a door to the Enchantment, a land with magic so coveted by this Grand Magician he'd heard so much about. Things were going his way.

Later, from a Tinabulon side street, Arthur, Beige and the others entered the trading post through the back entrance to find Aliena, Merlin and now Modred standing near the doorway. Modred tried to hide his cocky grimace. This bizarre band was the best Arthur could do? Merlin, however, saw other things in the newcomers and smiled. Aliena reacted with disappointment. She expected more solid warriors to join the cause. Instead there was the very young woman who had introduced herself as Devlin, a tiny Asian wearing strange armor; and the other woman, Harper, didn't look much like a soldier either.

Stellar, Jorn and Wolfer moved inside where they were joined by Jobie but the newcomers, unsure of their welcome, stood by. Beige grabbed Aliena in a bear hug and swung her around. Arthur tried to be patient as Beige said with pride, "Well, we made it back, little general, and with some top-notch fighters, too."

Aliena was taken aback, but gracefully extricated herself from Beige's grasp. "So I see. Xander's also called in his people. Our numbers grow."

Arthur moved forward, took Aliena's hand and again lightly kissed it. Beige noticed that she blushed, and he frowned. He and Arthur obviously had the same thing in mind, just different styles. "My lady," Arthur said, "I hope our long absence didn't distress you. We've collected a worthy group."

He didn't release her hand, and his touch obviously still unnerved her a bit. "I...uh, <u>we</u> were starting to worry. Garrum units have been prowling the town all night." "Yes, we know. We had a bit of an altercation with them earlier," Arthur informed her.

Aliena took her hand from his grasp and became the gracious hostess, addressing these new "guests."

"Welcome. Fleya will find food and a resting place for you. Thank you for joining us." Fleya pleasantly smiled and guided the new recruits further into the trading post while Aliena took Beige aside and spoke through her clenched teeth. "Could I speak to you privately, please?"

Beige shot a one-upsmanship glance at Arthur, who bowed to Aliena and joined the recruits. Modred followed him.

Aliena encouraged Beige to follow her away from the front counters. In the back storage room of the store, surrounded by crates, boxes and jars on shelves, Aliena and Beige sat down. He was a bit uncomfortably close. "Look Connery, I don't mean to criticize or sound ungrateful, but a midget and a little girl...?"

"Harper? She's got her rocket-daggers. I can personally vouch for her..."

Aliena shook her head. "No, the very young one, carrying the powerhead."

"Ah, she's called Devlin, and a devil she is. Deceptive exterior. She fought like a wild thing and saved Artos's life when we ran into trouble. She's no child." His eyes moved slowly over Aliena's body. "She can't be much younger than you. Judging by appearances, that is."

Aliena, still uncomfortable, stood and moved about. "If you say so. And the small warrior?"

"Shang is a wonder. We spotted a huge brute with a longbow and a battle-scarred face..."

She turned to confront him. "Well, why didn't you recruit <u>him</u>?"

Beige stood and moved forward until he was towering over her. "Because, my dear little general, Shang gave him that face!"

Aliena moved away. "Stop calling me your little general! I ask for soldiers and you bring me those Outlander losers!"

Beige walked to her, firmly placing his hands on her arms. "If we have any chance at all, it won't be with law-abiding storekeepers and farmers, or songbirds like you."

She tried to wiggle out of his grasp. "You shouldn't be surprised at how well I can handle myself in a fight. Now let go of me!"

"Artos and I have brought you survivors, people who, like you, live by their wits and weapons because they have to. We're damn lucky to have them." Disgusted with her attitude, Beige turned his back and moved away to sulk.

Realizing the truth of what he'd said, Aliena went to him and gently placed her hand on his shoulder. "You're right. It's not a time for peaceful scholars. Not yet."

Beige sunk deep in thought. "My father was a scholar... a scientist. A Garrum killed him when I was just a boy. I'll run into that one again someday...on my terms."

Feeling his long-held pain, she replied as he turned to her. "I'm sorry about your father. I suppose that's why you joined us then? For revenge."

Beige put his arms around her. "That's one reason." Before she knew what was happening, he kissed her, hard and deep. She felt it to her toes.

She slowly recovered and backed away. "Why did you do that?" She moved behind a group of crates, putting them between her and the amorous Beige. The cat-and-mouse stalk had begun. As they talked, Aliena continued to counter his moves toward her, all around the room.

"If I need to explain, then you've spent too much time singing and too little with your admirers." His wry grin further unnerved her.

"My songs have kept me alive."

She was nearing a corner. Beige saw his chance. "I remember one that almost killed you. Aw, come on, little general, take time to live a little." He lunged for her. She sidestepped and the crates clattered loudly to the floor.

Arthur, standing at the back of the store hoping to overhear the Aliena/Beige exchange, heard the clatter and rushed toward the storeroom door. Beige again had Aliena in his arms. She pushed him away and he tripped and landed on his behind directly under the shelves. Disappointed that the songsayer didn't encourage his advances, Beige yelled "Hey, keep your counterattacks for the Garrum. I saved your life, don't forget."

Aliena moved directly in front of him. "I owe you. Is that it?" Beige only smiled and shrugged. He slowly started to get up, eyes glued on her. Aliena scowled. She'd had it with this lover boy. As her hands folded into fists, a large jar on the shelf over Beige's head started to vibrate and shimmy toward the edge. Beige stood up just as the jar "fell" off the shelf, hitting him on the head and knocking him out.

Arthur entered abruptly with sword drawn. "Something wrong?"

Aliena was staring at the unconscious Beige and the shattered jar on the floor with puzzlement. Arthur's entrance snapped her out of it. "A misunderstanding, but thank you for coming to help." Beige groaned and Aliena and Arthur knelt beside him. His hand went to his aching head. "Gods! What hit me?" He saw Arthur with sword drawn. "I guess you're here to finish the job?" He looked reproachfully at Aliena. "I didn't think you had it in you, woman."

Aliena looked at the jar, still puzzled. "But, I didn't. It just... fell."

Arthur tried to help Beige up, but his aid was roughly shoved away. Once standing, Beige sized up the situation. He looked from Aliena to her "rescuer." They did make a nice couple. He suddenly slapped Arthur on the back. "Oh, to hell with it. I'll see you at the meeting." Aliena and Arthur, confused at the odd behavior, turned to watch him leave. What was that about?

Inside the trading post, Devlin had found a group of blouses for sale hanging on a clothes rack. She looked down at the tattered blue rag that was once her fancy, embroidered blouse. The girl longed for something pretty. Harper saw her sad expression. "They really roughed you up."

"My father gave me this for my seventeenth birthday two weeks ago." She touched what was left of an embroidered sleeve, a trail of yellow flowers cut off by an uneven hole. Was she on the verge of a good cry?

Harper guided Devlin to an alcove that had seating. She reached into her pack, pulled out a plain muslin blouse and handed it to the younger woman. "Here. Not as pretty but it's clean...ish."

Devlin took the garment gratefully. "Thanks." A stray tear ran down her cheek. She quickly wiped it away.

Harper tentatively asked, "So then your father died very recently at Garrum hands?" Devlin nodded. "And you killed three of the bastards?" Devlin nodded again with a faint smile at the memory. "Impressive", Harper replied.

Fleya brought two glasses of some kind of non-alcoholic liquid to the table. "On the house".

The women expressed their thanks. Harper wanted to know Devlin's story. "I'm so sorry. You can talk to me about it or just tell me more about you."

Devlin took a long slug of the drink. "My mother died when I was born. My father and I worked in the Grand Magician's stables, well, the Garrum stables, caring for the horses. Those bastards misused them. They were cruel. They were especially mean to my father." She paused. "I've seen you looking at my ears", she touched one of her scalloped earlobes. Harper protested. "I didn't mean..."

"It's fine. I know how...strange they are. My father carried more mutant genes. His ears, hands and feet were....different. You would think the Garrum guards, most of them look much worse, would sympathize, or feel a kind of brotherhood but no." Her forehead wrinkled at sad memories then she shook it off.

"I raised a colt; one who barely made it. Born early but he had such heart. I named him Strongheart." She smiled at that memory. "One day, we'd had enough mistreatment and so had the horses. We snuck out in the middle of the night, took the horses out of their stalls, drove them to the forested lands and set them free. Strongheart was out with a Garrum guard on patrol so we weren't able to..." She was close to tears again. Harper put a hand on her arm. "You don't have to talk if it's too painful."

Devlin took another sip of her drink and continued. "The Garrum tracked us to a canyon. They cornered my father. When he knew they were coming, he made me hide. They killed him for 'stealing' the horses. There were four Garrum. I was hiding high above and started a rockslide on top of them. That got three but one...got me." Her sudden smile seemed out of place. "But they never found the horses." She took a deep breath then looked quizzically at Harper. "Hey, now you. Why are you always so angry at Connery Beige? Were you...lovers?"

Harper took in a breath. This girl really knew how to cut to the chase. "We were...together. I wasn't that much older than you back then. I never knew my parents. I was sort of adopted by a caravan driver and his wife. They were actually good to me but, by my late teens, I was usually bored...and restless. Before he was ever the Marshal of a manorhouse, Connery led his Foresters in raids on rich caravans."

Devlin was learning forward now. Really into what, to her, sounded like a great adventure. "And they raided yours."

Harper nodded yes. "Beige hopped onto our wagon, saw me, grabbed and kissed me and my father would have lobbed a rocket dagger into his head if I hadn't jumped in front of him." She showed Devlin a glancing scar on her upper arm. "Wow", responded the enthralled young woman.

"So you saved the life of a guy who just appeared, grabbed and kissed you?"

Harper smiled very slowly. "He's a very good kisser. The Foresters took over the caravan but let my adoptive parents go. Except for a few fights and near misses, nobody was hurt. When they left with the goods, I went with them...with him. Over the years, I became a sort of honorary Forester, perfected my use of the rocket daggers but the fellows would most often leave me behind. Finally, the Garrum found their camp as the men were returning from a raid. I was the only one there. I saw Connery hiding in the distance and he saw me but he wouldn't risk exposing his men to save me. He mouthed 'I'm sorry', took them and left. I was able to get away on my own but I never saw him again until today."

Devlin was leaning forward on her elbows, head in hands. "Sooo, he abandoned you. Do you still love him?" Harper considered, remembering. "No. It was never really completely...right between us. I just like to give him hell for leaving like that." Both women laughed.

Chapter 15

In an isolated area near the trading post, Yaustis sunned himself in the dust rather like a large, very strange cat. Rolling on his back, he played with a glittering little silver object that looked like a flat whistle. His versatile eyes glowed a contented light rose. Nearby, Tiberius watched and muttered to himself. "Silly dragon". He went back to repairing one of the straps on his backpack. Padraig joined them, and Tiberius looked up grumpily. "You took your sweet time."

"So did the Council" replied Padraig, sitting down next to Tiberius on a large boulder.

Yaustis rose, flittered his small wings to rid himself of dust and joined them. "What was their decision?"

Padraig sighed in frustration. "They're doubtful any human could have the power to open the portals. We are to stay here until we can bring them more <u>facts.</u>"

Angry, Tiberius tossed his backpack to the ground. "We should stick with them rebels then but if that young 'un calls me 'monster' one more time, I ain't gonna be responsible."

Connery Beige, overhearing the exchange, joined the group. "Responsible for what, Tiberius?"

Yaustis resumed rolling in the dust to play with the silver, flat, whistle-like thing with his foreclaws. "He's just eccentric and too emotional. Pay no attention."

Tiberius pushed up close to Yaustis's large face. "Call me eccentric. You just about live by that caller. Won't let it outta your claws."

"I will so!" the thween replied as his eyes shaded toward red. "Here, Connery, you take it. A gift from me." Yaustis transferred the object over to Beige with a flick of his claw.

Beige examined it. "Silver?"

"Finest kind," replied Yaustis proudly.

"Thanks...for whatever it is."

"Take care of it. You may someday have need of it."

Inside Karayahn's stronghold, the Grand Magician sat at a huge desk in her chamber. Her right-hand lackey, Tryon, stood at attention at the door while the Grand Magician looked over a message on parchment.

"If this is true, Tryon, then we have an ally among the rabble...a very shrewd ally."

"Exalted One, what possible information could we learn from one of those wretched peasants?"

Karayahn rose and walked to her window, still reading the note. "Not a peasant. This is well-written and sealed in wax with a signet. We could gain the knowledge we prize most...the precise location of a portal to the Enchantment and the power we need."

Tryon dared to step slowly toward his ruler. "But, someone would tell you this?"

Karayahn rolled up the parchment and held it close. "For a price...to be named. He says he'll contact us. Meanwhile, he also writes of a band of rebels massing an attack. Puny, no doubt...a mere annoyance." She handed him the note. "See that the information is put to good use."

Tryon loved it when his mistress gave him any real responsibility. He smiled, bowed and backed out of the chamber. She picked up a mirror and examined her face; still attractive but were those new worry lines?

Scores of wary rebels entered the camouflaged opening of what might once have been a mine or, more likely a large, underground parking structure that, long ago, served a towering building. Now, it looked like an oversized storm cellar. The gathering men and women were Outlanders, wary but still willing to risk all on rebellion. The huge empty "garage" filled with rebels carrying various types of weapons, everything from clubs to high tech blasters. Aliena, Beige and Arthur stood behind a large, weathered conference table on a raised platform where they could be clearly seen by all. Katch and Merlin kept watch nearby.

The rest of the crowd stood divided into factions: Padraig and the Enchantment friends, Beige's Foresters, the new recruits and bands of scruffy locals. Everyone was talking at once and the noise was deafening. Beige motioned for Devlin, now wearing Harper's crème-colored muslin shirt and a pair of less-destroyed pants, to come up on the platform. He whispered something, and she smiled. She touched her powerhead to the ground, creating a loud bang and a charred hole in the ancient concrete. Shocked silence fell on the room, and all heads turned toward the platform.

Aliena stepped forward. "Welcome, everyone. We've a great task ahead, but together we can succeed." A general cheer went up, but there were overlapping comments from group to group. A shopkeeper taunted a Forester. "We don't need your kind. You stole from my warehouse just last week!" "That weren't us!", yelled Jobie.

A farmer fired his anger at Stellar Blue. "You bunch are no better than Garrum!"

A barkeeper walked up to Padraig. "You Enchantment types never cared what went on out here in the <u>real</u> world. Why should you start now?"

Padraig, Tiberius and Yaustis sadly reacted to the accusation. It wasn't that far off base. Padraig walked closer to the accuser. "We are all threatened by Karayahn. She wants to open our portals to get to power that could destroy both worlds. We've kept to ourselves in the past. Maybe that was wrong but now, with her knocking on our doors, we have to band together. Neither of our peoples can destroy her alone." The man backed off slightly.

Tiberius kept his voice down as he drew closer to Padraig. "Maybe our Council's doubts are makin' sense."

Aliena called for order by using a knife hilt to bang on the conference table. "Most of you know me." Another cheer and some wolf whistles went up, which Aliena acknowledged modestly. "Connery Beige and Artos here will form us into fighting units. Once we've stopped the Garrum Guard, we can stop Karayahn." More cheers went up while Arthur and Beige shared a doubtful glance. This was a tall order.

Another farmer stepped forward. "An' who's to run things once we've won? Mr. High-and-Mighty Marshal and his band of thieves?" The Foresters took offense and began to move on the man. Beige waved them back, and they reluctantly complied. Arthur's mind drifted back to his struggles to unite his own people, to the formation of the round table where all of his knights were seated equally. Could this camaraderie ever be recreated among these frightened, divided, far future citizens?

Aliena stood on the table so her strong voice could reach the back of the room. "Beige has suffered as you all have. Our future will be governed for the benefit of all and no one will be a pawn for the techno-wizards' amusement."

Another farmer had strong doubts. "It amuses me to stay alive. The Grand Magician's magic is too great."

The crowd seemed split in its reaction, some voicing agreement, some rebels ready to fight at any cost. Their voices rattled, roared and echoed in the room.

Aliena again raised her voice. "It isn't magic, but knowledge lost in the ancient holocaust. We can regain it, use it to build a future."

Merlin listened with interest, knowing that some power didn't rest in technology but inside the people who seemed least likely to wield it.

Stellar, hand on his weapon, was ready to fight. "Ah, we don't need these cowards!" The farmer group and barkeep reacted angrily, rushing Stellar. Wolfer and the others held them back. The general sound of discord rose again.

Beige turned to Aliena. "We couldn't form even a barroom mob out of this lot."

Watching the room disintegrate into chaos, Arthur shook his head. "They must first realize they share a common goal."

Aliena reached deep into her soul to pull out the obvious truth. "Freedom."

"What? Speak up", said a voice in the crowd.

Aliena spoke loud enough, even over the crowd. "FREEDOM!" Beige almost laughed. Did she actually think that would work? That only one word could unify? She was heard first by the diverse crowd closest to the platform who started chanting the word as others joined in, some with tears in their eyes, raising their fists and pumping them in unison. Before long, the whole hall rang with it, united...at least for the moment. Beige, impressed, sat down, realizing how jaded, even hopeless he had become.

Aliena's voice rang loud and clear again. "We will divide you into groups for training. Artos has led armies and Beige and his Foresters and others know how to combine older weapons with those we've captured and adapted. Together we can give the Garrum more trouble than they could ever imagine." Another rousing cheer went up.

As the crowd started to disperse, breaking into groups with more backslapping than insult yelling, Aliena took a crude map out of her traveling bundle and spread it out on the table, motioning for Arthur, Beige and Merlin to gather around. She pointed to various locations.

"This is Karayahn's fortress. It's formidable; but there are tunnels, part of an old system of underground travel, that I've reason to believe she hasn't discovered. Beige, you and your Foresters will train those with techno-weapons as well as bow and arrows. Artos, you take the fighters with more standard weapons; swords, spears, axes and the like. Here is what I want you to do. We have to put Karayahn's starcrystal out of commission."

Arthur and Beige exchanged a "wait a minute" glance. They weren't used to a woman assigning them duties and planning war strategy. Merlin smiled slightly. These men were underestimating her and they would learn to regret it.

Chapter 16

As the newly-united rebels continued to talk of weapons and training, a pair of rebel guards paced warily near the door. Suddenly, they were startled to have two contraction web grenades flipped in from outside to explode with soft thuds at their feet! Instantly, the webs sprung up around the men, the spidery threads wrapping around them and contracting. Both men fell, screaming and writhing. Hated Garrum officer Mekahn hurried in, leading a contingent of his guards. He pointed at an inner door which they blasted open.

Inside the meeting "hall," rebels, drawing their various weapons, scrambled as the Garrum smashed in. Beige's laser gauntlet took down several Guardsmen.

Devlin and Modred stood back-to-back protecting each other. She punched out with her powerhead while he wielded his sword with speed and accuracy, both of them dropping or wounding attacking guardsmen. Modred had no idea if the Grand Magician would take his "bait". Meanwhile her Garrum had no clue that they might be attacking an eventual ally. He reasoned that he could fall as easily as any rebel.

The Foresters whipped out their individual weapons and moved to form a protective wall in front of the platform. A Garrum struck the outspoken farmer before he could even turn in defense and the man dropped dead instantly.

"No freedom for him, poor sot", Jorn muttered while stabbing a Garrum in the leg.

At the conference table, Aliena quickly rolled up the map, stuffed it into her bag and motioned toward the back wall where a pile of crates were stacked. She waved Arthur, Harper, Katch and Merlin after her. Shang followed them. Quickly, she shoved the crates aside revealing a tunnel through the thick walls. She moved aside to let the others in obviously intending to stay back but Arthur grabbed her arm and pushed her into the tunnel. She started to protest but he shook his head and pointed into the tunnel. Her shoulders sagged but she acquiesced and followed the others. Merlin stopped just inside the opening, concentrated, made a delicate hand motion and the tunnel seemed to disappear as a vision of piled-up crates replaced it.

"Uh, I don't want to know how you did that but how long will it last?" Harper inquired.

"Not as long as it once would have but it'll buy us some time." replied the magician as he hurried her down the tunnel after the others.

Beige and the Foresters had formed their own defense line retreating steadily toward the tunnel and preventing any Garrum from getting close to it. Glancing back, all were confused on seeing the stacks of crates rather than an opening. Swords flashed in the low light clashing with soaring, flaming arrows from arrowlock launchers. Wolfer drew back his bow and precisely placed an arrow between facemask and neck of a Garrum about to kill a storekeeper. The Guardsman gripped his neck and fell backward. The rescued man quickly nodded his thanks. The battle continued until, finally, at the entrance to the hall, Mekahn slipped in behind his Guardsmen. He looked around quickly and spotted something odd on the rear wall. He blinked his eyes, clearing his head. Was there a pile of crates seeming to fade then reappear? What strange magic was this?

"Platoon A, follow me!" he shouted and traveled toward the rear of the room. A group of Garrum broke away from the fight to follow him. Gradually, the illusion cleared and the tunnel opening was obvious.

In the melee in front of the tunnel, Padraig, Tiberius and Yaustis formed a block. Padraig skillfully wielded his sword dispatching several Garrum. Tiberius caught another Guardsman's attention by poking him in the ribs with his short sword. The guard turned and Yaustis whopped him flat with his huge and mighty tail.

Yaustis sniffed derisively, "Rather unintelligent, these black-clad humans, uh mutants or whatever they are."

Padraig beat off another attacker as he snapped, "Agreed but never-mind. Into the tunnel!"

Slowly, the three backed toward the opening, holding off advancing Garrum. Padraig and Tiberius ducked in easily. Yaustis took one look at it, tucked and folded himself as small as possible and just barely managed to squeeze into the tight space. Weapons at the ready, the group began to back along the long, narrow tunnel route away from the fight.

Out on the floor, a small squad of rebels still held out against the advancing Garrum Guards. Xander used his blaster fiercely, trying to protect Fleya who wasn't doing badly wielding a spear but more Garrum moved toward them. The loving couple exchanged a knowing, last glance. A Guardsman ruthlessly cut them both down with his arrowlock launcher. Beige turned and promptly nailed him with a blast from his laser gauntlet. As the guard fell, other Garrum started to close in cutting off Beige, Modred, Devlin and the small group of remaining rebels from a tunnel escape. "Close it up! Close it up!" Beige shouted. Bitterly, the rebels bunched together to fight to the end.

Mekahn's voice boomed over the battle noise. "Take them alive!" Even more Garrum moved into position.

Beige looked up and, seeing that the group was hopelessly outnumbered, sighed and put down his laser glove. Those around him saw this and reluctantly began to lower their own weapons. Modred put down his sword and Devlin relinquished her powerhead. Why die in a useless battle when living to escape and fight another day was the better option...Beige hoped.

"Hold them here. Platoon B, after me! That tunnel has to emerge nearby", Mekahn growled. A small group of Guards followed him out of the underground "hall" and into the darkness.

Outside, in the rubble-strewn area where Shang was first seen, broken sections of ancient buildings provided some cover as Aliena, Arthur and the others moved debris, emerged from the tunnel and retreated toward the desert. Mekahn, spotting them in the moonlight, led his Garrum, coming at them overground.

Arthur, Harper and Shang formed a defensive line while the others moved on behind them. A Garrum arrowlock missile was launched, hitting Arthur's arm, grazing it. Would he ever get used to these other-worldly weapons? He ducked as one of Harper's rocket-daggers imbedded itself in Mekahn's thigh, bringing him down.

Roaring in frustration, Harper tossed Arthur her spare blaster. "Your pig sticker's no good for long-range work, Artos!"

Arthur hesitated, sheathed his sword, then brought up the blaster and fired it awkwardly. He was amazed and gratified when a Garrum guard fell. He might learn to appreciate these future world weapons after all! Harper grinned at him, then they both turned their attention back to defense.

Darting into a natural cul-de-sac formed by old, tumbled, broken structures, Aliena, Merlin and Katch tried to ditch three Garrum following them. They sheltered in an entryway, and Aliena activated her laser spinwheels but Katch and Merlin saw the Garrum getting out their contraction web grenades. With all his might, Katch stared at the web grenade in a Garrum's hand and concentrated hard. Merlin saw what the boy was trying to do. The grenade cylinder flickered, but did not disappear yet the brief flicker in and out of existence was enough to startle the Garrum who yelled, jumped and dropped the grenade without activating it.

Merlin gave both Katch and Aliena a light shove. "Good lad. You are getting stronger. Now get out of here, both of you." They made a break for it and Merlin gestured at the Garrum who pitched grenades after Katch and Aliena. A band of bright light conjured up a sparkling wall between the grenades and their targets, bouncing the weapons right back at the Garrum. As the contraction webs thudded open, the Garrum were caught in their own trap. They fell, screaming in pain, fear and astonishment.

Merlin quickly joined Aliena and her brother and the trio rounded a corner only to find themselves cut off by two more Guardsmen whose arrowlock launchers were aimed directly at them. Above the Garrum rose an ancient, two-story wall with some large pieces of broken masonry jutting over the top. Desperate and not really that aware of her own actions, Aliena spotted the pieces and closed her eyes. Her hands balled into fists as she concentrated. Her nails dug into her palms but she ignored the pain. Large pieces of masonry started to move ever so slightly. Suddenly, they jerked forward and fell, crushing the two Garrum where they stood.

In her faraway chamber prison, Lady Greer had been napping. She sat straight up in bed. Her eyes popped open, and she put her fingers up to her head as if in pain. The "vibes" subsided, and Greer began to smile to herself with hope flaring large in her eyes. She had hoped for so long. Now what had seemed only a faint promise of a living heir seemed strong and real.

No longer pursued, Katch stood staring in awe at his sister. Merlin had seen all and smiled at her. Aliena came out of her trance-like "concentration", opened her fists and her eyes. He palms were bleeding.

"Do you know what you just did?" said Katch, wide-eyed with more than usual excitement. "You moved those stones with your mind and made them fall on them. You saved us!"

Merlin moved in to give Aliena an uncharacteristic hug. "There it is, girl! The strong magic I knew you had inside you!"

Aliena looked at the downed Garrum and raised a hand, confused at the blood running down her wrist. "But, I don't really remember doing anything and I don't know how it works." Weakened, she almost stumbled. Merlin caught her.

"You will," Merlin said. "You will."

Sounds of a running fight grew louder. "We have to get to safety while we still can," Aliena snapped, her trance thrust aside. "Come on!" She wiped her palms on her shirt. Truly becoming the warrior in charge, she led them quickly with purpose, through the ruins.

As the night deepened, weary rebel survivors gathered around a cozy campfire. A pot of stew bubbled over the fire. There were other fires in the background. The group was camped on a long, cracked concrete platform raised above a swift-flowing stream of water. At either end of the platform were tunnels leading far out of sight. This was once part of the London Underground, but no train or tracks remained.

Arthur, whose arm had been grazed by the arrow, was cared for by Aaron, the Forester with medical training of sorts. Arthur thanked him for his care which pleased the Forester. He was rarely thanked, even by his cohorts who thought that he should just know they were grateful.

Although many faces were recognizable, missing were Modred, Devlin and Beige. Aliena paced the platform, looking sadly at the remnants of her "army." They had fought well, but the cost was high. Wounded men and women lay everywhere. She came to the campfire and sat next to Arthur, Katch and Merlin, all looking much the worse for battle. Shang-Sui restrung his longbow nearby. Arthur was examining a blaster while Harper showed him how to clean it.

"So many wounded," Aliena said as she poked at the fire with a stick.

"Ah, but we dispatched a number of them, too, don't forget", Arthur replied while cleaning the blaster and hoping to get her spirits up.

Harper leaned forward. "Aliena, have you seen Connery?" She sounded a bit more concerned than a casual old friend would be.

"No, not since we were raided."

Wolfer stood nearby. "He was pinned down by the Garrum in the hall. We couldn't get to him. Devlin and one of your people were with him, the dark one. He's usually with you, Artos. He rarely speaks unless he's…"

"Complaining." Arthur found it easy to figure out who Wolfer meant from the apt description. So did Merlin. "Dred." The men shared a knowing glance.

"This shouldn't have happened," lamented Aliena. "That meeting hall has been safe for years. We were careful on entering. No Garrum were in the area."

Harper said what everyone was thinking. "Somebody ratted." Then, quickly, "It wasn't Devlin. She's too grateful to us for saving her, letting her…belong somewhere."

Arthur stood up and touched his wounded, aching arm. "If I understand what 'ratting' is, the possible 'somebodies' are endless. Many are missing. I'm sure some of the less enthusiastic locals have deserted." In his heart he knew that, somehow, Modred might be responsible.

Katch stood next to Arthur. "Well, I'll bet it was Beige. He was the Marshal of our Manor House, y'know."

Faster than her rocket daggers, Harper was up and grabbing Katch by the shirt, practically lifting him off the ground. "Watch your tongue, you little whelp or I'll cut it out!" Aliena stepped in, pushing Harper back. "No one really believes that. Connery told me about the Garrum killing his father. He hated being a Marshal. It couldn't be him." She wanted to be more positive than she really was. Harper backed off.

Padraig, very agitated, approached the campfire. His musical voice had lost its pleasant tone. "Aliena, friends, we are all in grave danger."

Wolfer casually stoked the dying fire. "Tell us something we don't know."

"What's wrong, Paddy?" Aliena stepped away from Harper.

"The plett. It's missing," said Padraig with the utmost concern.

Aliena and all the others looked puzzled. "The what?"

Padraig forgot, for a second, that he wasn't in the Enchantment. "You'd call it a key, I suppose. It opens all the portals to the Enchantment. Yaustis had it when we went to the meeting hall. Now it's gone. He might have dropped it in the fight, but I think someone took it from him. He's very upset.

In the distance. Yaustis huddled in a corner, very alone, defeated, forlorn and looking oddly small. His tail slowly swished back and forth making patterns in the dust. His colorful eyes were a deep blue.

Aliena understood. "One of the Garrum could have this key, and if Karayahn learned how to use it..."

Arthur continued. "The doors to the Enchantment would be wide open to her. Our 'rat' must have taken it." He looked thoughtful, as did Merlin. Who would always sell out for power? Of all Arthur's knights and old world associates, only Modred. He realized that the others knew nothing of his past struggles with his nemesis, nothing of Modred's true nature. No way could Beige be the "rat". Was bringing Modred with him and joining this rebel band going to be their downfall? Was he awakened only to bring destruction with him like a horrible plague?

Aliena looked as if she might collapse. "Then we're lost. Whoever has that key, controls both our worlds."

Feeling guilty, Arthur put his good arm around the heartbroken young woman. The rebels in the circle stared sadly into the dying embers of their campfire.

Chapter 17

The next day, on an open road under a blistering sun, a small band of rebel prisoners walked yoked together two by two with their hands tied behind their backs. Garrum, some on foot, others on horseback, escorted them. Mekahn, his leg now bandaged, traveled alongside in a horse-drawn, metal-clad wagon lording it over the small column. Several pairs ahead of Devlin and Beige, who were yoked together, Modred, the only prisoner walking alone, was being prodded by another Guardsman. "Leave me alone you hulking idiot!" For that he got a blow to his head with the butt of the guard's blaster.

Beige, also angry at his capture, bore visible bruises and a couple of burns left by arrowlock missiles that grazed him. Devlin limped a bit but when she slowed down, a Guardsman gave her a jab with a sparking electronic rod. She looked as if she might collapse. "What will they do with us?"

"Don't be stupid. If you were them, what would you do with us?", snapped Beige.

"That does not bear thinking on but they've kept us alive, hoping to get more details on the rebellion I suppose." She straightened. "Well, I will give them nothing." Beige was impressed with the young fighter's bravery as they stumbled on.

In the far distance, Wolfer watched through a cobbled together magnifying device as the Garrum Guards were seen making their way across the baked landscape on foot prodding rebel prisoners. Several transports were scattered about. The Garrum commander lounged in a wagon. The Forester couldn't make out faces.

Wolfer pocketed the device and stealthily slithered trough a jumble of broken slabs and pocked remnants of twisted steel girders to snatch a torch left on a wall. He fired it with a spark from a flint box and moved through a dark area of caved-in ceiling and down a flight of corroded steel stairs. His ancestors might have recognized this as an escalator very long ago. In the distance, the murmur of voices could be heard. He finally emerged on the concrete platform that was once a subway. Aliena and Arthur spotted him and came forward.

"They're out there and they have the prisoners. I can't tell if some of our numbers are among them", said Wolfer.

Arthur turned to Aliena, "Can they find this place?"

She reassured him. "Not likely. We only discovered it ourselves a few months ago, and only then because a slight earthquake uncovered the entrance." She called to her cohorts who moved closer. "Jobie, Harper. Keep watch at the entrance. If any of the Guards start moving our way, I want to know about it." Harper and Jobie hurried away, Harper automatically checking the status of her daggers as she went.

"What do you propose to do now, my lady?", asked Arthur slowly getting used to taking orders from this small but strong female.

"Fight it out here if we have to. They can't get more than one at a time through that opening." She paused considering. "We can't help the prisoners now, not and live. Our numbers are small as it is".

Wolfer returned having gathered Stellar and other rebels. They all faced Aliena and Arthur with expressions of doubt and more than a little regret. "Aliena, the others here want to talk to you."

Stellar stepped forward. "So, we've been talkin' and we think as soon as there are no Garrum in sight, we clear out too."

"And go where?", she inquired.

"The deep Outlands", he met her eyes. "We scatter and hide. They'll forget about us."

Aliena stepped closer to make a personal impact. "They don't forget. You know that. And, none of us has a chance alone."

Wolfer spoke with sadness in his voice. "We're no threat to them but we're a nice fat target if we stay together."

Small Shang pushed a few rebels aside to step forward. "The Garrum do not like the deep Outlands. They are afraid of the spirits there. Even the techno-wizards do not go far into that place. We can fade like spirits there ourselves."

Arthur had been listening in silence. He knew it was time to make his point or his return was useless. He stepped forward appearing larger than life in the torchlight. He rose to full height looking commanding, kingly. "And live to fight another day? There's only one thing wrong with that. Divide your force now and another day will never come. We've suffered heavy losses but what is left, <u>you</u> are the toughest, most deadly fighting unit Karayahn's army has ever had to face and there are still others among the people who would fight with men like you to train and lead them."

The rebel Foresters displayed a mix of pride and puzzlement. Arthur moved even closer to the fighters while Aliena made way for him. She had never heard him speak with quite such authority before. He explained. "Karayahn doesn't know exactly what attack we may mount against her or where. From this point on, we will let them make the mistakes. I've been in this position before."

"Where?", asked Stellar.

A brief memory clouded Arthur's thoughts. "The name of the place makes no difference. The situation was the same. I trained and led a core group of fighting men, turning the enemy's strengths against them. <u>And we won our freedom</u>."

"Why are you not still there now, Artos?" Shang asked quietly.

How could he explain the long story of his death and technical, magical rebirth? How could Aliena win her war without these fighters? "My work was done. Old soldiers move on to new battles." He raised his voice. "But, I tell you this. If you run now, you might be able to escape the Guard but you will be hiding the rest of your lives. Karayahn and her techno-wizards will have prevailed. She'll become even more desperate, dangerous and brutal as more of her so-called magical devices and weapons fail. If she gains control over the Enchantment she will only use the power there to make your lives even more miserable. You'll regret giving up the fight more than ever. He paused as he locked eyes with the rebels nearest him one by one. "You know this!"

Wolfer reacted to the strong words. "Duke, you sound like you know her."

Arthur thought back, picturing the faces of ancient enemies. "I've known many like her". He put a hand on Wolfer's shoulder. "So, do we cower in the far Outlands or fight her together?"

The fighters murmured amongst themselves as Aliena tensed, unable to sense whether feeling was turning among them. Stellar stepped forward, setting his shoulders defiantly. "I don't like running."

Wolfer shrugged. "Never thought much of it myself".

Shang tilted his head and smiled slyly. "I have always said it is better for me to see the back of my enemy than for him to see mine".

The murmur of assent rose. The tide had turned. Arthur's intervention had made a difference. Aliena grinned at him with appreciation and, perhaps more.

In a grimy, heavy stone dungeon, rebel captives were roughly shoved into small, dark cells. The ceiling was low and the walls close. They could be far underground. The only light came from a few dim, naked bulbs that occasionally flickered, failing as were many of Karayahn's marvels. Mekahn watched as a Guard locked the cells. Modred, nursing the bump on his head, was in one with two rebel prisoners. He rushed to the bars holding out a hand to Mekahn.

"Officer. I must see the Grand Magician". In another cell Beige and Devlin exchanged a sharp unbelieving glance. Mekahn snorted a laugh. "She will come to view your execution". He started to stride away.

Modred played his last card. "Officer, show Karayahn this. She will find it quite significant". There was a glint of gold in his cupped hand. Mekahn was about to use a powerhead on him but stopped to pick the signet ring from Modred's palm and examine it. He smiled maliciously. "She will still watch your execution. Scum!" He exited the dungeon followed by all but one of the Guards.

Beige and Devlin grabbed the bars of their cell, outraged. "Bastard. You and your friends betrayed us." Beige yelled. Modred ignored them and stood watching the outer door of the dungeon waiting for Mekahn's return. He was proud of what he had accomplished in this new world. He hadn't lost his edge. A nasty smile creeped across his face. "Correction. I betrayed you."

Chapter 18

Later, inside her posh chambers, Karayahn fingered Modred's signet ring, turning it over in her hand while looking out a window, her back to the room. "I have had the use of you, traitor. What further need do I have". Turning, she stared at Modred who, brought to her from his cell, stood near the door. He moved slowly toward her as he spoke. "These rebels are not my friends but you underestimate them. Their battle leader is a man unlike any your Guardsmen have ever fought."

The Grand Magician's interest was piqued. She had no idea the ragtag rebels had a leader. "Battle leader?"

Ah, he had sunk the hook. "Yes, an experienced soldier. If the rebels defeat your Guards once, they'll gain in numbers. Lose twice and you will face a vast army of rebels. But, I can help you. I fought and defeated Artos before...in other lands." He dared move closer. "With my help, you can snuff out the rebels like a candle".

She slyly smiled and moved a bit away. "How good of you to give your aid so generously. But...

Losing ground, Modred tossed out the last tidbit. "I offer more. I told you I know where one of the portals to the Enchantment is located."

She dropped the signet ring into an ornate dish on a table. This traitor to the rebels was of no real use. "Location is unimportant if we cannot open them."

Modred's slight smile was unsettling. "I have a key to unlock it. It could be yours, Grand Magician."

This was getting interesting. She lifted her heavy skirts and walked up a few steps to a throne-like chair so that she could look down on him. "In return for what?"

He moved in quickly, sitting on the step below her perched like a vulture ready to circle its prey. "My life and an opportunity to destroy my enemy, battle leader Artos. And if I prove my worth to you, perhaps you will find some part of your kingdom I might govern in your name."

She considered. Trust was never one of her strengths...or flaws. She wasn't stupid enough to ever trust this slimy traitor but she was weary of prodding Lady Greer to open a portal. "A very reasonable offer. I accept. Where is this key?"

He stood. "No my lady. I am not fool enough to have it about me. It is hidden, far from here. I will fetch it when there is need of it."

"That will be very soon", a very thin smile pulled on her mouth. He smiled back, just as thinly.

In the dungeon, a lone guard stood watch near the door away from the cells. Beige and Devlin huddled in a corner of their cell. Other prisoners lay weak and dispirited paying no attention. Beige surreptitiously reached down and twisted the heel of his boot, removing a thin wire with knotted ends. The boot also contained a gold piece which he took out and handed to Devlin while sliding the heel back into place.

"Get the guard over to the bars." She looked at him with a "who me?" expression. "You're just a little girl. How can you hurt him?" Ah, right. She shuffled meekly to the cell bars looking as defeated and weak as she could manage.

"Lord Guard. Some water? Just a few drops of water?" While Beige moved along the cell wall out of the Guard's sight, Devlin dangled the shiny gold piece so it flashed in the light. The Guard took notice, hesitated then walked toward the cell. She waited until he was close to the bars and angled so his back was to Beige then she "fumbled" the coin, dropping it into the cell. The Guard, intent on the prize, didn't notice Beige, behind him, reaching his arms through the bars, the thin wire between his fists.

Beige whipped the wire over the Guard's head and yanked it tight. The Guard dropped his powerhead to claw at the wire around his throat. Beige yelled at Devlin. "The powerhead!"

Devlin reached through the bars and grabbed it as the Garrum struggled but finally slumped and Beige dropped him. As he stepped back, Devlin blasted the cell lock open. Beige bent over the guard relieving him of his bandolier of contraction and hot web grenades while Devlin blasted open the cells of the other prisoners. Beige handed some of the grenades to them, leaving Devlin with the powerhead.

"Follow me", Beige ordered. "Devlin, cover the rear. If anybody falls out or gets lost, he's on his own". The others nodded their understanding and Beige led them out, moving as quietly as possible. In the depths of this stronghold corridor, Beige ghosted along stealthily, the others following.

In the dark lower corridors, bulbs had flickered out creating only patches of light. At an intersection, a Garrum Guard passed by. Beige and the others hugged the wall but the scuff of their feet was heard causing the Garrum to return, arrowlock launcher ready. Beige deftly flipped a contraction web grenade at the Garrum's feet. It popped open with a soft thud and the webbing snapped up around the Garrum's body instantly contracting and shriveling and before he could scream, Devlin blew him away with the powerhead.

"Nice teamwork" Beige cracked a smile toward the tough young woman. One of the others helped drag the Guard into a side corridor and Beige picked up the dropped arrowlock launcher as he waved the others after him again.

From the base of a winding staircase with the same murky lighting, Beige led the prisoners up with Devlin bringing up the rear. As bad luck would have it, the rebels encountered a group of Garrum coming down and, after a mutual moment of shock, Beige grabbed the lead Guard's arm, yanking and toppling him down the steps where he landed at Devlin's feet. She quickly blasted him and one of the other prisoners snatched up the launcher he dropped along with his bandolier of web grenades. In the meantime, Beige used the circular wall as cover and lobbed hot web grenades toward the Guards above then motioned Devlin to join him.

"We'll have to rush them". Devlin fired back with "Retreat isn't in your vocabulary is it?"

"I get bored seeing the same thing twice" and with that the ex-Manor House Marshal fired a volley of arrowlock missiles at the curved wall opposite him producing a hail of ricochets up toward the Garrum killing and wounding them. Clever, thought Devlin. Beige led the charge up the stairs firing and two Garrum fired back hitting two prisoners before ducking into a room off the landing and slamming the heavy door. Beige led the prisoners past the door toward the top of the stairs where there was another weighty door. This one was unlocked so Beige motioned his cohorts through then locked the door behind them.

Suddenly, everyone was on the roof in eerie starlight. Devlin looked over a low wall to the ground, very, very far away. There was a peaked, slanted section of roof on one side, the waist-high wall on the other. No escape.

"And so it ends". Devlin slumped down to sit, leaning against the wall. Beige motioned to the others to sit down, out of sight from anyone below.

"Maybe not". Beige extracted a flat, silver whistle-like object from a concealed holder inside his belt. "Yaustis gave me this. He said it was a caller.

"That dragon? Who...or what does it call?"

"Let's find out". He blew the thing but no sound was heard. Devlin shook her head. "It's broken".

"Maybe it only works in the Enchantment." He blew another soundless blast on the thing as pounding on the door racked everyone to attention. Devlin and the last two prisoners turned, weapons up. The heavy metal door began to glow in the center from heat weapons aimed at it from the inside. Beige, Devlin and the others waited, weapons ready. On another section of roof, a door flew open and Mekahn and a group of Garrum came through, advanced over a flat area then began to clamber over a peaked section. They slung their weapons awkwardly, forced to use both hands to climb.

"They're up there." Devlin had detected the scrabbling sounds to their right and poked Beige. "Right", he replied. "You men use hot webs first. Try not to waste them."

The men nodded and got set, facing the slanted roof, using some ventilators for cover. As soon as the first Garrum helmets rose over the roof ridge, the rebels let go with arrowlock launchers and hot web grenades.

A few Garrum were hit and rolled down the slanted roof, their bodies thudding below. Mekahn angrily gestured more "cannon fodder" into position. Beige, Devlin and the others fired and lobbed grenades at them as they fired back. The hot webs exploded around Guards wrapping them in deadly flaring webbing.

One of the grenade-hurling prisoners was hit by Garrum arrowlocks and fell dying. Devlin grabbed his stash of grenades and tossed them one at a time toward the enemy. The door near our rebels was glowing red, starting to melt!

The only surviving rebel prisoner was felled by an arrowlock missile and seconds remained until the red hot door would be breached. Devlin and Beige exchanged a frantic glance. He squeezed her shoulder. "I'm proud to have known you." She smiled "Same here." Breaking the moment was a whooshing sound from above. All turned to look upward and the Garrum ceased fire in puzzlement then open-mouthed shock.

A large shape blocked out part of the stars. Then it settled lower, revealing itself to be Yaustis. "You called?"

Beige and Devlin stared astounded at the thween lowering himself gracefully toward the roof edge. He craned his head down at them curiously and continued. "Don't you want to get out of here?"

"You kidding?", Beige leaped forward followed by Devlin. As they clambered onto the thween's back, Mekahn recovered and aimed his arrowlock launcher, shouting to his men, "Fire! Fire!" Just then the melting metal door was breached and more Garrum rushed through.

Mekahn shot and missed as Yaustis, his eyes an agitated bright yellow, lifted off and soared away while missiles flashed close around him. Angrily, Mekahn waved at his men to cease firing. "Enough! They're gone."

A confused Guard asked his commander, "What was that thing, Sir?"

Mekahn stared at the now empty starscape. "I'm not sure but I've seen it before."

"It was Yaustis the thween". Modred was in Karayahn's chamber a bit later. The report of the winged rescue had reached them. "Aiding these rebels", he continued.

"We must begin our invasion of the Enchantment at once", answered the ruler. She paced toward a window to look up at a still starry sky. Were more dragon-like creatures up there?

Modred felt the time wasn't yet right. "There is time, my lady. The three from the Enchantment said they are only scouts and there is more than one Enchantment portal. We would be wise to locate any others before planning an invasion."

She moved away from the window, drawing drapery to shut herself off from any prying, enchanted eyes.

"Agreed. Nonetheless, you will bring me the portal key immediately".

Modred smiled and bowed graciously. He had the monarch hooked. "As you will".

Back on the ancient, wrecked subway platform, Forester Stellar bolted in from guard duty outside, his face alight. "Yaustis is back!" Aliena, Arthur and others followed him rushing toward the entrance where they heard the flapping of many small wings and saw the thween settling to the ground lightly, Beige and Devlin sliding from his back. Beige turned back to address his "ride". "You shouldn't be able to do that you know...fly".

Yaustis wiggled, fluffed and snorted. "Neither should bumblebees. But, then of course, <u>they</u> escaped from the Enchantment in the first place." Beige smiled and nodded. He didn't know that. The thween found a quiet corner and curled up to rest as his eyes settled on a calm, sleepy, light blue. Flying humans around was a bit exhausting. His large eyelids fluttered then closed.

Aliena, Arthur and the others came out of the narrow entrance. Jobie, Jorn, Aaron and Stellar immediately knew to post themselves as lookouts while Aliena ran toward Beige and Devlin, throwing her arms around them both. "You're alive!"

Devlin grinned and Beige hugged Aliena back enthusiastically. "Thanks to Yaustis and his caller."

Arthur strode up behind them. "And what of Dred?" Beige stopped hugging Aliena and slowly turned to face him. He didn't answer but jumped for Arthur's throat. The two men crashed to the ground struggling while Aliena tried to pry them apart. "Stop it!" They continued to struggle as Arthur rolled on top of Beige, trying to pin him. Beige freed an arm and sent a looping punch to Arthur's head. Aliena grabbed a blaster from a Forester's holster and ran forward to level it on the combatants.

"I said, <u>stop it</u>!" She fired a blast into the ground. Beige and Arthur slowly pulled apart and rose as Aliena gestured "up" with the weapon. "Connery, what's going on?"

The men straightened their clothes as Beige answered. "Ask him. Ask him about his traitor friend".

Aliena lowered the weapon. "Artos?"

"He's not a friend. I would guess he has allied himself with Karayahn."

Beige moved closer to face Arthur. "You guess right Duke. He was imprisoned with us and admitted it. And why should we trust you? He came here with you."

Arthur muttered, mostly to himself, "I'm sorry. I would have chosen another if I'd had the ability" then, raising his voice. "Look, Merle and I are still here, not with Karayahn. We are at your mercy if you choose to kill us." Merlin nodded in agreement. Modred was bound to keep true to his unfortunate character.

Beige took a deep breath. "Because I was Marshal of a manor house there are those who called me traitor but you put the real traitor among us!" Arthur hated his old nemesis even more for this recent betrayal. "We fought by your side and I intend to keep on doing so...if you will let me". He looked from Beige to Aliena. Beige quickly looked toward Aliena. "It's not my decision".

Aliena weighed the situation briefly, then nodded "Yes. We need you." She locked eyes with Arthur. Was this response more personal under the surface?

Beige straightened his weaponry, slowly accepting her decision. "Right. Dred knows where this hideout is. We've got to move before Karayahn's troops get here. We don't have much time."

"Is there another sanctuary?", Arthur inquired.

"I know of more", Aliena replied.

Later, when the Garrum Guards rushed in ready to blast anything that moved, the place was deserted.

Chapter 19

As Beige and Devlin joined the others at Aliena's suggested new sanctuary for a war council, Harper spotted her Ex and smiled. He had beaten fate yet again. But, as she approached him, she wiped that friendly welcome right off her face.

"Really didn't expect to see <u>you</u> again." Beige grinned and approached her. "Not that easy to put me in a grave. Besides, I had help". He gestured to Yaustis who had again tucked himself small in order to sit at the war council makeshift table composed of two time-damaged marble benches with a thinner marble slab placed over them. Harper took in the tightly tucked Enchantment resident. "Who would've thought that...critter would have a braver heart than most of us?" Harper spotted Devlin and came forward. The women shared a welcome back hug.

As he took a seat, Beige looked around. They were in a once cavernous basement housing a great many crated objects. The crates and many of the items inside had fallen to dust, except a classic Roman marble statue and a mummy case, suggesting the vast basement storage area of the British Museum.

In this place and time, it was clear that Aliena was at the figurative "head" of the table and Arthur sat next to her as her key soldier. Beige sat on her other side. Merlin, Harper, Padraig, Tiberius, Yaustis and Devlin inhabited various mismatched stone remnants they'd rolled up as chairs. There was a low din of chatter. Aliena cleared her throat and then...silence.

"What does Dred have to bargain with…aside from what he knew of our location and plans?" Yaustis carefully leaned forward. "There is the missing plett?" Padraig finished the thought, "And if he has it, he must know how it works by now and where the Tinabulon Portal is".

Aliena frowned. She looked defeated. "Then there's nothing to stop Karayahn and the techno-wizards from attacking the Enchantment." Arthur put a hand over hers on the table. "Except us".

Tiberius rolled up a larger stone seat to make him as tall as the others. "You keep forgettin'. The Enchantment is not gonna just lay down y'know. The Council is darn worried about the portals, remember?"

Yaustis moved a bit to get more comfortable bumping aside the severed head of an ancient statue. "Tiberius, the last time the Mid-Eve Council moved fast was right before the Ice Age." Yaustis and Padraig exchanged knowing looks.

"I might be able to make them see reason. After all, I'm an Enchantment general myself." Padraig announced.

Tiberus slumped a bit. "You and Yaustis go. I'm not so good at politics and these guys here'll need some extra help".

Arthur spoke with authority. "In the meantime we will have to form some kind of defense in front of the portal."

Harper tried to be logical. "Just one question. If you have to have one of those plett things to open the portal, how are you two going to get in?"

Yaustis smiled, in his own fashion. He preened his wings and wiggled one of his foreclaws. "There are ways…"

Later, outside the Tinabulon Portal, Yaustis sketched a mystic diagram in the air with his claw. The cliff face shimmered and became opaque clearly outlining the large portal. "See, nothing to it", bragged the Thween. "Finally, your ability to pick a lock actually means something", Padraig fired back as the duo moved through. The portal quivered and splintered around their shapes then shimmered back into an ordinary cliff face again.

In a damaged alcove of the ancient museum, Arthur sat honing the sword he had carried since the cave. Young Katch warily approached the once and future king. "I want to help. You didn't see what my sister did to some Garrum", he moved in closer almost whispering. "She can move things with her mind but it scares her. I'm not scared. Ask Merle. He's helping me make things disappear."

Arthur put his sword aside. "So he tells me. Magic must run in your family. You just need help developing it." Katch sat down next to him and Arthur put his arm around the boy's shoulder. "We need all of our warriors. Your time will come". "Yeah? When?", Katch sighed impatiently, stood and walked away.

Poof! Merlin suddenly appeared beside Arthur who raised an eyebrow. "That is a risky trick, you know. If someone saw you, you might be taken for a techno-wizard". Merlin snorted. "It's one of the few things I can still do...and their techno-wizards can't. The world is in a shabby state with no real magic in it. Aliena and Katch have power, probably inherited but they lack the skill yet to use it properly."

He gathered his cape about him, sat down comfortably and indicated Arthur's sword. "But magic or not, in the end, everything always comes down to that."

Arthur picked up the sword and ran his hand carefully down the blade. It was sharp enough now. "So it seems." He sighed. "I wish Excalibur were with me. Is it destiny Merlin? That I was brought back to fight a hopeless battle and that Modred returned to betray us...again?"

His old pupil was discouraged. "Destiny? It doesn't apply to you. It doesn't matter who set you down here, Arthur. <u>You</u> will decide what path to take...and how to walk it." He placed a reassuring hand on Arthur's arm. "You see, some people find a star to follow. You <u>are</u> that star."

Arthur let out a brief laugh. "And Modred?"

"Modred has never looked up at the sky in his whole life. He is the center of his own limited universe." The wizard slowly got up. "Well,

I'd better be going." And he abruptly popped out of sight. "Merlin…" Arthur wasn't finished talking to his old friend.

"Hello? It's just me", Aliena was picking her way through the museum debris toward him. She smiled and indicated the sword in his hands as she sat beside him. "That's such a limited weapon, Artos. Why don't you carry an arrowlock launcher? Or at least a blaster?"

He smiled. "I am more comfortable with this."

She looked down with a frown. "I'd die so we could have a world where we didn't need weapons at all."

He remembered his own goals so long ago. "I would say that is worth dying for."

Aliena nodded slowly and hesitated then said awkwardly, "Artos, sometimes, well, I still feel I dragged you into this. You never really said you wanted to take on the Grand Magician and her army. You could've gone far away from our rebellion or be working for a rich caravaner…" She considered her next statement…"Or made a wealthy marriage. You came out of nowhere, like magic."

"You have your own magic. Don't be afraid of it." He tried to reassure her.

"I don't understand it. I'm afraid I'll misuse it."

He turned her to face him gently grasping her arms. "You won't. I know you and this is where I should be. I chose it freely, Aliena. I have taken this fight for my own, though I cannot explain all the reasons why…except that you are one."

She blinked. "Oh?"

He continued. "You have such…spirit…such courage." She brightened and he let her go. Arthur didn't pay as much attention as he should to how his words affected her. He was looking back at other times and other people now. He shifted, toying with the sword again.

"I had a lady once…she had spirit and courage too. My wife…

Aliena was visibly affected but he wasn't looking at her then. "Oh", she said flatly.

He continued with his story. "I had her loyalty but her heart belonged to another man. I had his loyalty and...he had my wife."

"Is that why you traveled so far? To leave them behind?"

Was that a small tear in his eye? "They have both been dead a long time."

She wasn't sure how but she seemed to know that "a long time" had been centuries. "Oh".

He pulled himself out of his sorrowful recollections. "But you are very different, Aliena. Your whole heart and devotion are to a higher cause...and it is one I believe in too." He took her hand in his large one, placed it on the hilt and crossguard of his sword and raised them as he kissed her hand. She stared at him, astonished, moved and hopeful. "Oh".

Inside the Enchantment, the Mid-Eve Counsel met in their chamber that night. This was an oddly nebulous realm made of light and shadow, color and shifting fog. At the center of the room was a huge, glowing free-form table. A number of beings were seated around it; small elves like Tiberius, homely trolls, tall, slim Gentry like Padraig, exquisitely beautiful water sprites, a giant, pixies who had the disconcerting habit of shape changing at odd moments and fairy hags, hideous of face but delicate of form.

Seated on two handsomely-carved and slightly raised thrones were Titania and Oberon, Enchantment royalty. Both were tall, graceful and strikingly attractive with dark sloe eyes. Both were dressed in lush green and gold.

Padraig and Yaustis sat to the side and below the thrones. Yaustis inhabited an oddly-shaped chair that fit his huge form perfectly. Most of the company listened with some interest to the sonorous speaker, a heavyset elf named Bailin who swayed gently back and forth as he droned on. Padraig and Yaustis were irritated and Padraig's long fingers tapped impatiently on the chair arm. Yaustis curled and uncurled his tail (the equivalent of clenching his fists, if he had any).

"…And I must remind you I was not in favor of a delegation going through to the Real World, even on such an important matter as the portals, and you can all see what contact has accomplished. We are asked by our esteemed colleagues…" Bailin nodded to indicate Padraig and Yaustis. "…to become involved in a RealWorld struggle that is none of our…"

Padraig angrily surged to his feet. "It isn't a matter of whether or not we want to be involved! The techno-wizards have the key to one of our main portals and their army will assault it, possibly within hours." This racked everyone to attention.

"The only thing standing between them and us is a small band of ill-trained, ill-equipped Humans who care enough about freedom to stand in our defense. No one asked them to do it. They volunteered."

Bailin moved forward. "Even so, I must remind my esteemed colleague that there are certain parliamentary procedures for calling up the armies of the Enchantment. They cannot be circumvented." There was a loud murmur of agreement and "Hear Hears" from the Council. Even Oberon and Titania seemed inclined to agree. Padraig slammed a hand down on the table angrily, causing a whisp of fog to quickly exit the area.

"Then you follow those procedures and Bad Cess to all of you." The Irish-rooted curse was rarely used and had its effect. "I'd rather fight beside Duke Bellorum and the others than stay here with the likes of you!" Yaustis fluttered his feathers as his eyes darkened. "And I".

Oberon frowned and stirred, holding up a hand. "One moment. Padraig. Who was it you would rather fight beside?" Padraig turned to his King and proudly stated, "Artos, Duke Bellorum".

Oberon seemed a bit shaken, his response tentative. "Might he also be called Arthur, Dux Bellorum?" Around the Council chamber heads came up sharply, all attention on Padraig's reply. Padraig cast a puzzled glance at Yaustis, then, "He introduced himself as Artos but I've heard Merle call him Arthur". Titania turned to her mate. "And Merle? Merlin?" This put a new spin on things.

Chapter 20

Inside Karayahn's Chamber, Modred held the key, the plett, its round, blood-red stone looked very unprepossessing. He extended his hand to offer it to her. She eyed the object with suspicion. "You could have picked that up beside any road."

Modred looked at the odd object closer. "But I did not. I picked Yaustis's pocket for it."

Karayahn's nose curled up in disgust. "Yaustis is the...thing?" Modred dared to correct her. "Thween". Karayahn picked up her skirts and started pacing. "How could such a creature have pockets?" He followed her around the room. "My lady if you believe the creature exists, you must also believe it has pockets. This plett is the key to the Tinabulon Portal."

She stopped cold, causing him to almost run into her. She turned and took the plett, turned it over in her palm, then clutched it in sudden triumph. "Come with me. There is someone who must see this."

Karayahn, followed by Modred, stormed toward Lady Greer's chamber. The few birds nesting in the corridor ceiling took flight in fear. The ruler told the guard at the door to unlock it, failing to announce her visit. Greer sat in a comfortable chair idly humming to herself, playing cat's cradle with a string. On seeing the ruler, Ona bowed low toward her and her strange guest but Greer paid no attention to them and continued with her string. Modred walked around the chamber looking with interest at various objects until Greer finally glanced up at Karayahn.

"Come play with me?" Was she only pretending to have regressed to a childlike innocence?

Irritated, Karayahn thrust the plett into Greer's face. "No, I'm not playing any more games. I don't need you now. My friend here has brought me this...the key to the Tinabulon Portal to the Enchantment."

Greer's eyes slightly widened but she managed to control a horrified expression. At the dressing table, snooping Modred stiffened as he saw something. He jerked around toward Karayahn.

"Lady Karayahn, this symbol..." He pointed to the symbol on the mirror base which lay exposed. Karayahn briefly glanced his way.

"It's the lady Aregnan's family mark. What of it?"

Modred slyly smiled. He might be providing more information to cement his place with the ruler of this strange new realm.

"I've seen it before. It is carved into the head of Aliena's lyrit." Greer slowly rose. Her pretense of madness was gone. She was intent only on this information and damn all else. "Who is this Aliena?"

Karayahn was irritated. "Nobody really. She is a songsayer, the girl who leads the rebels against me". Greer flashed a look of triumph to Ona and straightened fully to face her captor.

"Not just a girl, Karayahn. She is the heir of Aregnan."

"Ridiculous", snapped the ruler. "The Aregnans were exterminated root and branch twenty-four years ago...except for you."

Greer dared to move a bit closer. "No. There was a child, newborn to my cousin's wife and smuggled out of the stronghold just before it fell."

Karayahn began to pace again. She touched the symbol then whirled around to face Greer. "No one escaped that massacre."

Now Greer's true family pride resurfaced. "Three tried. Ona's son and his wife and the baby." Ona bowed her head as she remembered. "We were never sure if they got out safely. The only Aregnan possession they took for the child was the Prince Elector's lyrit, the one this man saw."

"Aliena said she'd always had it", said Modred.

"It's impossible", Karayahn replied.

Greer, feeling her true strength for the first time in eons, proudly touched her fingers lightly to her temples.

"I've reached out with my mind. I felt someone...I could only hope...now I know she is there and I've kept you out of her world all these years by pretending to be mad." Greer smiled. "I've beaten you, Karayahn and my young cousin will now know who she is".

Furious, Karayahn reached into her robes, pulled out a small laser derringer and fired, close-range, at Greer who gasped as she was hit and crashed to the floor instantly dead. Ona, sobbing, sat and pulled her close.

Modred took this as a great exit cue. "I will see you on the field of battle Grand Magician." With that he bowed and left in haste. Karayahn sat down unsteadily. Yes, another Aregnan was eliminated but what of this young songsayer/general? Lycenia Karayahn instantly hated her for many reasons. She no doubt had enormous psychic energy powers. The Grand Magician could only hope that she didn't yet know how to use them well.

Little Lycenia was born with powers as well. Her father was an officer of the Aregnan court and a very distant cousin of that once ruling family. But, was the birth of his girlchild welcomed? Never. Her mother was a Juventius; the one family that the Aregnans never truly made a lasting peace with. Her father had done the honorable thing when not allowed to marry her mother; he'd provided for Lycenia, given her and her disgraced and disowned mother everything...but his love and acknowledgement. In truth, he did love them but lacked the backbone to cross his family. He never possessed the courage to openly accept his paramour and her offspring.

As she grew, it was obvious that the child had inherited a few meager powers. She could move small things with her mind and mend objects she had accidentally broken, thus often escaping punishment.

When her mother died, Lycenia was whisked off by the Juventius family to a sort of posh orphanage to be hidden and forgotten. There she learned to hone what powers she possessed. By the time Lycenia was a young teen, she could impress and even terrorize fellow "orphans" who picked on and teased her.

At age 16, she was apprenticed to an isolated but well-to-do household on the edge of the Outlands. The baron, head-of-household Walker Karayahn was a valued and, at that time rare, techno-wizard and the pretty, dark young woman, working as a maidservant, observed him and his work at every opportunity, learning the combination of science and "magic" that would one day serve her well.

It was there that she met the Baron's son Hadrick, a semi-handsome 19-year-old whose cruelty was matched only by his raging ambition. Lycenia's dark side appealed to him and they found each other sexually exciting. The young couple ran away, were married and with a populace determined to avoid war at all costs and a fortune that Hadrick had stolen from his father, were quite easily able to set up a formidable estate and recruit a large, protective, mostly Mutant force that would later become Grand Wizard Karayahn's Garrum Guard.

Always with the goal of destroying her father's disapproving family the Aregnans, Lycenia tried to turn her husband against them but without success. He was too busy amassing a greater fortune as a successful "fixer". Want someone to disappear? Hadrick Karayahn was your man. Want a caravan robbed and put out of business? Look no further. Eight years into their marriage, the childless couple's usually sizzling sex life cooled beyond repair and, seeing no further use for her husband, Lycenia poisoned him, setting up an ambitious guardsman to take the fall as his killer.

It was almost simple to build her protective force into the Garrum Guards and, without much resistance from a still docile peasant populace, join forces with other wealthy, if shady non-royals to overthrow the House of Aregnan, move into their castle stronghold and emerge, eventually, as The Grand Magician, feared if not respected throughout the known lands. That was twenty-four years ago. Now, with techno-wizardry unsuccessful at finding or creating another starcrystal, a failure to penetrate the Enchantment's gates and a struggle to just keep the lights on in her own stronghold, all the once untouchable ruler needed was a power-packed Aregnan heir to rally the people against her. She had never wanted the last of that cursed family dead more in her life.

At the same time, in the ancient museum hideout, the object of the Grand Magician's wrath, Aliena played her lyrit, plucking out a tune for Katch's entertainment although she was clearly worried and he was still concentrating on Artos' rejection of his fighting services. Suddenly, she stiffened and the instrument fell to the floor. "Aliena!", shouted Katch as she crumpled and he jumped forward to cushion her. Merlin, Arthur and Beige rushed in, Arthur easing her weight from Katch and lowering her to the ground. Beige whipped off his jacket and made a pillow to prop up her head.

"What happened Katch?", Arthur inquired.

The songsayer's little brother looked terribly worried as he picked up the fallen Lyrit. "I don't know. She was playing and, all of a sudden, she sort of froze up and then she just fell over. What can we do?"

Merlin moved forward and checked Aliena's pulse, heartbeat, eyes, etc. "She's in a trance".

Katch was a bit freaked. "I don't think she's ever done <u>that</u> before." Right then Aliena twitched and moaned slightly. The men bent over her attentively as she slowly blinked open her eyes as if coming out of a deep, dreaming sleep. Her face had a new maturity and awareness as she looked up at them. Beige moved closer. "Are you alright?" "Yes. Yes". She held out her hands to be helped up and Arthur and Beige jumped in to do the honors.

"What was it, sister? What happened to you?" Katch asked as she studied him with a new attention and some sadness. She put her hand on his head. "It was a voice...a woman's voice thundering in my mind. She said I was the heir to the throne and said she was my cousin Greer."

Beige was shocked. "Lady Greer" But she was killed with all the other Aregnans."

"And we haven't got any cousins." Katch insisted.

"You haven't, Katch", said Aliena touching her head. "She told me so much in a huge burst of energy. It's hard to work out but Mother and Father weren't my parents. My real father was the Aregnan Prince Elector. They smuggled me out of the stronghold and raised me. You're their child, Katch...but I'm not."

Aliena seemed a bit woozy. Arthur guided her to sit on a nearby piece of rubble that must have once been an impressive, carved bench. Shattered, Katch rushed up to sit at her feet. "No! It's Karayahn who's making you think that!"

Aliena reached out to comfort him. "It was Greer. I'm sure of it. Karayahn held her prisoner because she thought Greer could open the Enchantment portals. She could but she wouldn't. A few minutes ago, Karayahn showed her the key, the plett. Greer has been feeling my presence and she sent me her last message to warn me...as she died."

Beige's face tightened in anger. He knew that the Aregnans were honorable and fair rulers long ago. "Karayahn murdered her."

As Aliena sadly and slowly nodded, Arthur felt her anguish and tried to comfort. "She must have been a very honorable and gallant lady. I think it runs in the family". Aliena and Arthur exchanged a long glance that made Beige uncomfortable because of its great warmth.

Katch frowned as a realization and a new question hit him. "Aliena, if, I'm not your real brother then why can I sometimes make things disappear? I don't have your powers but I guess I have...some."

Aliena moved closer to him. "You ARE my brother in every way that counts and the Aregnans aren't the only family to control psychic energy. There have always been others. The Aregnan rulers were always the most powerful and, of course, well-known. Once Karayahn took over, those with any powers at all judged it best to keep them hidden.

Merlin stood at full height and cleared his throat. "Then isn't it time the heiress to the throne started gathering her army?" Aliena rose up and was standing straight and strong.

"Yes. Connery, Artos, draw up the line of battle and get them ready. There is a field nearby, hidden by debris and trees. You can train them there. I haven't seen a working drone in more than a fortnight. It's unlikely that the Grand Magician will be flying any to search for us. Connery, gather the fighters. We won't have much time now."

Arthur promptly bowed his head as he brought his closed fist over his heart. "Yes. Your Highness". He turned and strode away. Beige looked in astonishment from the departing Arthur to Aliena, then pulled himself to attention and duplicated Arthur's salute. "Right away uh, your Highness."

Aliena approached Merlin and, almost whispering, "Merle, as you've heard, the Grand Magician has a machine. It has destroyed entire settlements with one blast. She will use it in battle. I fear that nothing we have can destroy it. I've seen your magic. If there is any way for you to get close enough to do it damage, that might turn the tide for us."

The ancient magician nodded. "And I've seen your magic even if you aren't, as yet, able to fully control it. Katch is learning. Perhaps together...?" Aliena smiled and nodded back at him.

Katch stood miserably beside Merlin wondering what his part in this great rebellion would be. Aliena noticed and went over to the boy, gently touching his face, lovingly moving a piece of stray hair out of his eyes.

"I have a problem, Katch. I don't want you hurt and I can't leave you behind. Will you stay close to Merle and help him?"

Katch knew Artos had said he must learn more in order to help but beside Merle maybe he could learn "on the job". "You mean that?" His grin lit up the cavernous room. "I can't let anything happen to you. You're all the family I have." He threw his arms around his sister and she hugged him tightly as an approving Merlin moved away.

Chapter 21

Under cover of deep night, Foresters Jorn, Jobie, Stellar, Wolfer and Aaron were on a mission to quietly sneak up on a platoon of sleeping Garrum to steal as many techno-weapons as possible. Training would be useless if the rebels couldn't adequately arm the fighters. There was plenty damage to be done with bow, arrow, axe and spear but a farmer with a powerhead, now that was more like it.

Outside an old stone barracks, a snoring Garrum with a badly disfigured, mutant face was leaning against a wall. Wolfer, Aaron and Stellar crept stealthily inside the sleeping quarters while Jobie distracted the lone guard by picking his pocket as Jorn clubbed him and stole his powerhead which he placed in a large, leather sack he carried specifically for weapon gathering.

Inside, Stellar poked Wolfer to get his attention when he noticed that the sleeping Garrum, all tucked neatly into their racks, had leaned many of their blasters, arrowlock launchers and powerheads against a wall and placed web grenade belts in a large box for the night. The men grinned. So convenient!

Aaron stuffed as many loose grenades and belts as possible into his carry sack while the other Foresters went for blasters, powerheads and launchers. Everyone froze when a falling blaster slid along the wall to tap the ground. Several Garrum were semi-awakened and began muttering their irritation but quickly went back to sleep while the Foresters exited as quietly as they entered only now, armed to the teeth.

The same operation was duplicated successfully at a Garrum camp-gound only a shoot-out proved necessary when Jobie tripped in the dark over a large tankard tossed aside by its drunk owner. Luckily, Foresters were able to kill or badly injure the Platoon of Garrum before they could exit their bedrolls and a smooth get-away was accomplished.

At one point during the night, Aaron and Wolfer located another Garrum barracks next to a stable and made off with not only a pile of web grenades and blasters but two war horses! Jobie, Jorn and Stellar hit the jackpot when they got a tip from a storekeeper that a stockpile of techno-weapons was kept in a bunker nearby. The lone Garrum Guard dozing out front was an easy mark and the Foresters' large, leather sacks were bursting at the seams by the time the first rays of dawn appeared on the horizon.

"Seems these Garrum badly underestimate us", Jobie commented while mounting his horse.

"To their future deep regret", Jorn yelled over his shoulder as Stellar led them thundering away to impress Beige, Aliena and Artos with their success.

With the pilfered weapons and more distributed among the rebel, would-be army, training sessions began on the well-hidden field near the ancient museum. Beige and the Foresters chose a bar owner who was already proficient with bow and arrow to train men and women to use them with humans as targets rather than the usual animals in-tended for supper. Harper and Shang-Sui trained another group to shoot straight and strong with bow and arrow and arrowlock launchers. Gradually, arrows hit center target more and more with a few excep-tions that almost embedded themselves in passing Forester flesh.

Arthur, Padraig, Tiberius and other rebels used to wielding sword, axe or spear, guided increasingly competent commonfolk to poke impressive holes in hastily-constructed targets representing close-up, hand-to-hand enemies.

For more high tech close-up action, Aliena teamed up with Beige to instruct on the use of the laser gauntlet and her spinning laser knives which had to be employed with great skill lest the user cut off his or her own wrists.

Arthur allowed Beige to teach him to better aim and reload a blaster although he would always prefer using a sword.

Devlin and Jobie worked with fighters carrying powerheads and, while one rather clumsy fighter almost blew off his own foot, the two saw definite improvement as the days wore on.

Wolfer and Stellar taught combat on horseback using spears and also found that tossing web grenades could prove more viable from the back of a horse.

On the sidelines, Merlin helped Katch use his talents to make objects temporarily seem to disappear. The boy concentrated on a sword lying on a bed of straw. He struggled.

"I can't! Nothing is happening." Katch stomped a foot and began to stalk away.

"You have the ability, boy. Have faith in yourself. Believe!" said Merlin as he guided Katch back to where he formerly stood. "Picture it gone. See nothing but air in its place."

Katch closed his eyes and balled his fists. On opening his eyes and with a new determination, he stared at the sword. It flickered then, seemingly, was gone! Aliena's brother beamed at his teacher as the wizard gave him a hug.

One morning with training in full swing, two men were crawling on their bellies through rubble and foliage until they were within decent viewing distance of the action on the field. Modred and Tryon, who was far overdressed for the mission and complaining each time a random branch poked his delicate skin, stationed themselves at the edge of the field hidden by a large, broken wall. Modred withdrew a crude sighting instrument from a pack at his waist and used it to bring the combatants into focus. He had a nice view of Aliena spinning the laser knives at her wrists.

"There she is. The last of the Aregnans. I must say that, with those spinning knives, she is rather impressive."

Tryon reached for the "scope". "If the Grand Magician had let me focus more of our remaining power on repairing the sky drones, we wouldn't be crawling out here in this rubble." He swatted at a flying insect that kept attacking his face. Looking through the sighting device, Tryon focused on Aliena. "Hummm, pretty thing but hardly a battle general."

Frustrated that Karayahn made him take this pompous ass along, Modred grabbed the scope and searched the field to settle on Arthur who was impressive in a mock swordfight with a peasant while Foresters and others watched intently. "Not her! _Here_ is the battle general!" He passed the scope back to Tryon who looked where Modred had pointed the device.

"Oh. I see. Well...that's unfortunate." Tryon frowned as he looked around the field to see rebels well-armed and effective with both standard and techno-weapons. "There are more of them with more weapons than I anticipated and they're actually quite...good."

Modred sighed, pocketed the scope and turned to slink away. "I was afraid of that. I've learned the hard way that one can never underestimate Arth....uh Artos. I've faced him before."

As the men stealthily exited the edge of the field and made their way through the surrounding woods, Tryon remarked, "Yes. So you've said. You'll have to enlighten me and the Grand Magician with more details. We're still a little foggy on your past."

Modred just smiled. He had no intention of revealing any more of his history and certainly not to this bootlicker.

"That explains why several of my Garrum barracks were hit by ex-Marshal Beige's Foresters." Karayahn, Tryon and Modred were in her courtyard where she stood under a large shade tree. "I assumed those thieves were just arming themselves to better attack more rich caravans." Tryon followed a short distance behind her as she paced taking care to leave room in case she stopped short again. She responded with irritation shooing him away. Modred sat on a nearby stone bench.

"We will have to take the Tinabulon Portal to the Enchantment by sheer force", he said with authority." There are more portals but dividing your army into small attack groups now could mean disaster if the residents of the Enchantment are ready for us." Karayahn moved to stand before him. She didn't like this outsider dictating battle strategy to her. It was as if Modred were her ruler and not the other way around. He continued. "There are only three beings from there who have joined the rebels but they've made at least one trip back inside. Who knows what forces they've convinced to join them."

To equal the playing field, Karayahn sat down next to him, her anger building as she leaned in for effect. "<u>You</u> advised me to search for other portals. Now you tell me we've allowed time for the rebels to build a formidable army!"

She had him on this point. With Arthur's battle skills and the addition of Aliena to spur rebel loyalty and fighting spirit, it was too late to expect only an ill-trained, ragged force to serve as enemy.

The Grand Magician calmed herself and considered her options. "Without the participation of Enchantment forces, we have a good chance at victory. Enchantment royalty has always been more than reluctant to meddle in our affairs. It is doubtful that three of their scouts could convince them to do so now."

Modred stood, looking down at her, hoping to regain a little control. He knew it was risky to raise his voice. "Do you want to risk everything on that assumption? Your devices are failing more and more. Tryon here tells me that your supreme weapon is weakening." Tryon looked a bit frightened as his eyes widened in a 'Who? Me?' reaction. The Grand Magician cast him one of her best evil eyes. "And that crystals in the Enchantment are the only source of such strange power", Modred continued. He was on a roll. "Yes. I might have underestimated the enemy but if you want to take the power you need, you can't afford to wait any longer, not with the army Artos, their battle general has built!"

Karayahn stood and stalked away from him to stand on a slight rise. She suddenly seemed very far away. "I don't care about your general nearly as much as I do getting rid of this songsayer. I'm told that she is the 'heart' of the rebellion." The ruler looked into the distance. "Once she is dead, we will see how much longer their general can keep up rebel morale. Very well. Gather our forces. We will wait for them by the portal".

Chapter 22

Stretched out on the Tinabulon plain, under a bright sun stood Karayahn's massive, impressive army. The Garrum Guards were separated into several commands, infantry armed with arrowlock launchers; Mekahn had a regiment of Garrum using launchers which spit out the deadly heat-seeking web grenades. Modred commanded a squadron of mounted Garrum equipped with powerheads. Tryon headed a small battalion of techno-wizards assigned to guard and operate the star-crystal machine which was secured to a mobile platform in the army's midst. It was huge. Its crystal center was the size of a two caravan wagons end to end. This was the only position with which Karayahn trusted him. Even those under his command knew they were really on their own.

The rebel troops were a smaller, tense group of perhaps five hundred in all. Arthur carried a blaster but kept a sword at the ready as he commanded a cavalry unit. Beige was in charge of most of his Foresters who seemed to be armed with every weapon they could find. Harper and Shang shared command of a group of archers. Jobie and Devlin led a platoon of "pikemen" armed with powerheads and tri-staffs. The others were spread out among these basic divisions. The faces of farmers, storekeepers, craftsmen and women alike reflected purpose and unity along with a good dose of terror.

Tiberius and Padraig were with some of the rebels they had trained in the use of sword and spear. Yaustis was oddly absent from the field of battle.

"Do ya think the Council will see fit to bring our forces to the party?" Tiberius was hopeful but had his doubts. He had come to this strange RealWorld as a scout, to learn who was tampering with the portals to his world and here he was armed for what might well be a hopeless battle.

Padraig gripped the hilt of his sword perhaps too tightly. "Yaustis must have gone home for one last appeal."

Tiberius snorted a semi-laugh. "Or else he's sittin' all cozy in a crystal field sippin' his favorite nectar while we're out here dyin' with this lot." He looked around at the frightened but hopeful rebel troops. Padraig thought more of the thween than that but even he had his doubts.

Aliena, Merlin and Katch stood directly before the cliff face that housed the Tinabulon Portal to the Enchantment. Katch was busy making a tiny flower at his feet seem to disappear. It did so quite quickly. His skills had improved. Merlin sensed Aliena's fear but felt her determination as well. "Remember girl, there are powers inside you. All the strength of your Aregnan clan through the ages is with you today." She knew the truth of the wise magician's words but wondered if she'd be up to the task. At heart she was a songsayer, an entertainer, the keeper of legends set to music. What strange fate placed her here at the head of a perhaps doomed rebellion? She looked over the vast field at her forces standing firm in front of a massive death machine. Her eyes settled on Artos, the mysterious battle general who showed her such kindness and loyalty. He seemed to sense her gaze, turned and the two locked eyes. There was a bonding, a heat that was both supportive and thrilling. Her lips pulled back a bit and the two shared a small, encouraging smile.

Beige walked his mount over to where Arthur sat his horse. The once and future king was back to coldly studying the army arrayed against them, in particular, Modred's cavalry. Grim history repeating itself. He still wondered if he was too "soft" in awakening his traitorous nephew when he should have killed him where he lay. Certainly he'd been too optimistic in the hope that, in such an altered, new world, Modred might reign in his vast ambition. Now some of these unfortunate rebels would no doubt pay for Arthur's error. Should he and Modred come face-to-face, he would have to make up for his poor decision with laser weapon or sword and he was ready to do so.

"You ever seen anything like that before, Duke?" Beige tried not to sound anxious.

Arthur paused before launching a litany. "Glein, Dubglas, Bassas, Celyddon, Castellum Guinnion, Urbs Legionis, Tribruit, Agned, Mons Badonis..."

Beige was a bit dumbfounded. "What's all that?"

"Battles I've been in."

"Win any?"

Arthur's war experiences flashed before his eyes. He smiled very slightly. "All."

Beige frowned, impressed. "Where DO you come from? I never ever heard of that many battles!"

Arthur shook off his reverie. "It doesn't matter now. It is...past. But Dred remembers them as well as I do and I know what he's sitting there thinking."

Beige looked again at the vast threat before them. "So, he'll have a defense."

"Yes". The comrades in arms studied the army which was now slowly advancing on them. Beige took a deep breath as he weighed his next words carefully.

"If this is one that we don't win, Artos, just want you to know that wherever you come from, we, uh, I'm glad you're here. And, you and our little general...I think there's a future there."

Arthur smiled briefly at the thought. "There is much you don't know Connery but I thank you."

Modred rode over to Karayahn who stood on the starcrystal machine platform. He pointed off toward the rebel lines.

"The portal lies there, my lady, in the cliff behind the rebel line." The Grand Magician was looking through a hovering set of binoculars that self-adjusted to bring the distant cliff into sharp focus. Evidently one of her few high-tech gadgets still in working order.

Karayahn pushed the binoculars aside, removed the plett from a pocket, aimed it toward the portal and activated it. It began to glow and throb with a crimson light. Across the plain, the portal shimmered and outlined itself in the cliff. Shifting colors chased across the opaque surface. Staunchly facing the enemy, the rebel fighters ignored the action at the portal but Aliena, Katch and Merlin stepped back unaware that Karayahn's use of the plett was the cause.

The Grand Magician was awed by the portal's response. Modred nodded at her with the characteristic evil grin and, as though awaiting applause, "The Tinabulon Portal, my lady."

She ignored his bravado, nodded back briefly and stepped higher on the platform to be seen by her commanders. Activating a small audio-com unit...

"Attention all commanders. Our goal is before us. We will enter the Enchantment and take what we need. This gathering of riffraff is of no consequence. We will easily win the day!" To this the Garrum and a few techno-wizards responded with cheers. She continued. "Initial bombardment will begin on my mark! Five-four-three-two-one-MARK."

Mekahn's Garrum fired their grenade launchers. A group of techno-wizards blazed away from camelback turrets which were essentially laser guns operating link mini-guns. Rarely seen in Arthur's England, camels, with guns to boot, were a bit disorienting to Artos and Merle.

The rebels reacted as these first shots missed or fell short but the firepower was awesome. Many rebels were shrinking back in the face of it. Where had the Grand Magician been keeping these bizarre beasts? War was something their ancestors spoke of but it had been centuries since the great war that destroyed the "Old World". The small scuffles between barons, both robber and Wizard-backed, were mere barroom brawls compared to this terror. Arthur and Beige called in encouragement, reminding the fighters of their training and steadying the lines. Then the full battle was on them.

Harper and Shang's archers calculated the angle and distance and their longbows rained a lethal shower of arrows on the steadily-advancing Garrum. The arrows, reinforced with armor-piercing heads, arched high and descended. The Garrum began to fall as the arrows found their targets. Mekahn roared in anger. How could such a puny group do him any damage? He directed his Guards to concentrate on the archers.

The camelback turrets fired with a regular, sweeping action, mercilessly devastating the front line of defenders. Merlin quickly went into action making a few magical passes in the air at the camels. The beasts bearing the turrets began to sag to their knees and keel over...sound asleep. The techno-wizard operators jumped off furiously trying to rouse them and get them back into firing position again. It didn't happen. The targeted rebels laughed and cheered at the small victory.

The starcrystal machine started to glow and hum until its ray lanced toward the rebels. Abruptly, the machine faltered and the ray died. The techno-wizards were aghast as Karayahn screamed at them. "Fix it, fools." They quickly clustered around the device, fiddling with various controls.

Several rebels noticed and were astonished. They had finally seen this legendary, horrific weapon fail! Beige, the Foresters, Padraig and Tiberius ran forward under the cover of a new hail of arrows from the archers to engage the Garrum grenade launcher operators and infantry in close combat.

Modred's cavalry stood two-deep in a close-packed line. Arthur and his riders moved forward and were joined by a group of late-comers who, as planned, were charging out of a near-by ancient subway tunnel. They joined Arthur's line and spread out to start their charge. Modred reacted to this addition to Arthur's forces but, as always, his cocky pride didn't let him feel any effect. Then, Arthur's riders began to pull toward the center, finally forming a flying wedge bristling with powerheads and laser weapons on its outer edges. The wedge smashed through the center of Modred's line, firing as they went. For a time Arthur had Modred in the sight of his gun but his well-aimed shot was quicky blocked. Riders on both sides fell.

Taking advantage of the surprise Arthur had sprung, Jobie and Devlin's rebels ran forward, using tri-staffs and powerheads on the disorganized Garrum riders. Aliena ran toward Merlin. "Merle now! Can your magic stop that machine permanently before they start it up again?"

The wearied magician raised his hands to start a spell. "I'll try." Out of nowhere an arrowlock missile slammed in and took him in the side. He fell, crying out. Aliena and Katch rushed to him. He was nearly unconscious but he grasped Katch's shoulder firmly. "You do it, boy."

Katch was panicking. Merlin drew him closer. "Make something on the machine go away..." With that, Merlin fainted and Aliena bent over him administering primitive first aid until Aaron rushed to assist with limited but often effective medical care. Katch screwed up his face in concentration, staring at the frightening machine. In the distance the techno-wizards had succeeded in getting it to start again. It hummed and glowed and the ray was ready. Karayahn smiled in satisfaction as the ray stabbed out, catching a small group of rebels and rendering them into screaming mounds of dying flesh.

Arthur's men swung around, gathering their mounts for another wedge-charge back through Modred's cavalry. Modred, cursing, gathered his people around him, waving them closer. Beige, the Foresters, Tiberius and Padraig were going hand-to-hand with the Garrum infantry. Without a pause, Jorn flung himself in front of an arrowlock missile aimed at Beige's back and collapsed, dying against his leader and friend who screamed in horror and anger. Shattered, Beige had little time to do anything but note where Jorn fell and keep on fighting. Wolfer jumped in, blasting the Garrum Guard who got Jorn then went on covering Beige's back. Stellar, in tears, fought beside him.

Aliena and Aaron had roughly bandaged Merlin but he was barely conscious now. Katch still tried to "vanish" something on the Machine, angry at his own inability to step up when it counted. Aliena bent over Merlin, her courage wavering. "They've got us, Merle." She looked up at her brave warriors giving their all when defeat seemed imminent. Merlin squeezed her hand.

Jobie was ridden down by a Garrum cavalryman and fell but took the Garrum with him, using his tri-staff as he toppled. Devlin ran to stand over him and fight off the attackers but there were too many and one finished Jobie off before he could rise. Devlin saw that she could do nothing more for her fallen comrade and quickly spotted the dead cavalryman's horse. She ran toward it and grinned in recognition. It was Strongheart! She'd know him anywhere.

"Old friend! Thank God!" She lept on his back to escape.

Modred had pulled his remaining cavalry around him, even though Jobie and Devlin's rebels harassed them with powerheads. Arthur's wedge charged again and his riders thundered back through Modred's defensive square firing laser blasters. The deadly starcrystal ray caught some of Arthur's cavalry, narrowly missing him. There were few men left now. Arthur pulled his mount around and saw the open portal glittering ahead of him. Had the Enchantment abandoned them? Was he a fool to expect their interference in RealWorld affairs after all?

Something was moving inside the gate; something in the mystical fog. Suddenly, a human arm, feminine, strong and clad in iridescent, white Irish moiré silk reached through the opaque gate and extended a familiar, much-loved, bright sword toward him...Excalibur!!

Arthur's face lit up as he spurred his horse toward the Portal with a whoop of triumph. On the move, he cast away his laser blaster and far inferior sword from the cave. Aliena's saddened eyes were following the action. His victorious yell made her curious as he grabbed up the enchanted sword from the feminine hand. She had no idea why he was so affected by this offering from the Enchantment but his joy was enough for her. Then, gradually, her eyes brightened as she remembered the lyrics of an old, legendary song about a "Once and Future King". She was finally putting all the pieces together.

The arm retracted behind the portal and it cleared as something never seen by human eyes came charging out.

Yaustis, red-eyed, flew through leading a flight of fire-breathing thweens, looking for all the world like a squadron of ancient world B-17s. Close behind, on ground level, thundered the Gentry cavalry mounted on the hell horses of the Wild Hunt, fire-eyed black chargers that struck sparks with their hooves as they galloped. Padraig was jumping up and down at the sight. "I knew it!" He picked up the diminutive Tiberius who, at first, objected but then went along for the "ride" as the much taller man swung him around.

"Well, the Council must've listened to reason after all", he responded. "Put me down ya big oaf!" Padraig did so but only after planting a big kiss on his fellow scout's dirty, blood-stained cheek.

Stinging fairy darters were zinging through, striking for the vulnerable points in the Garrum armor. When an impressive elvish infantry poured after the Gentry cavalry, Tiberius ran toward them and joined their ranks. The commander of the Gentry cavalry rode up to Padraig leading an impressive fire-eyed charger behind him. "Command is yours, sir. After all, we are your unit." Padraig grinned and gave the horse a pat. "How are ya Demonus? Did you miss me?" The horse neighed a response and his pawing hoof created a mass of sparks as the tall Gentry leader swung up on his back and led the glittering, otherworldly cavalry into the thick of the battle.

The enemy, Karayahn, Tryon, Modred, Mekahn and their mutant horde reacted in astonishment and some fear as they saw the on-rushing Enchantment forces. Karayahn snapped around to the machine operators who had stopped working the apparatus. "They can't stop my Machine! Use it now!" The Techno-wizards quickly put it back into action and a ray stabbed into the elvish infantry annihilating a swath.

Katch, seeming to have grown up overnight, never giving up, despite the spectacle before him, sweated in concentration still staring at the starcrystal. Instinctively he crossed his fingers and suddenly the huge crystal vanished, completely and for real, not just a seeming, cloaked version of gone! The Machine stopped. Karayahn furiously whirled on the techno-wizards. The chief operator was nearly in shock. "The crystal's gone. It just disappeared." He moved his hands over the empty space that the great crystal usually occupied. Katch opened his eyes, delighted. "Hey, I think I... It's <u>really</u> gone!" Merlin yelled. "That was always the final goal. Now, concentrate!"

Katch was wavering. The crystal was dimly reappearing, then gone again. When a few stray enemy Garrum approached to stop Katch, Aliena revved up her wrist laser knives and quickly dispatched them. When she saw Katch's concentration continue to waver, she, although still unsure of her newfound power, stepped in concentrating. The platform on which the machine stood creaked backward a tiny bit, then forward making any true aim very difficult.

Led by Yaustis, red-eyed thweens went after the machine platform and techno-wizard attendants. Yaustis scorched Tryon with a fiery blast. Okay, yes, thweens, like dragons were capable of a fiery breath. They were just reluctant to use it. They hated the comparison. Tryon collapsed in flames. Never able to wake their sleeping camels, other Techno-wizards deserted the turrets and tried to run as thweens pursued them. On the machine platform, the wizards were frantic. Why was the crystal starting and stopping its reappearance. What was shaking the platform under their feet? Whose magic was this?

Mekahn directed his Garrum against a surge of Foresters and elvish infantry. As he stood in the defensive line, an arrowlock fired by Wolfer tore across his chest, ripping open his breastplate and the jacket underneath. Beige paused staring. Mekahn's chest showed an old scar extending from left shoulder down and across to his lower right rib cage.

Beige's vision reeled as, even in the hell of this battle, his mind returned to a devastating past incident. A flash of brilliance strobed in a tunnel. Men were yelling, fighting. There was a black-armored and helmeted Guardsman, a middle-aged civilian and a teenaged Connery Beige. The Guardsman killed the civilian with a powerhead and the boy looked down in horror as his father fell. Young Beige reached down blindly, snatching a laser knife from the dead man's hand. He struck like an adder, stabbing at the Guardsman, raking the hot knife across his chest from left shoulder to lower right rib cage. The Guard fell back looking down at the steaming wound while screaming. Here, now, the old would was revealed. Beige's rage matched that of his youth. "It's you. You murdering bastard!"

He moved in closer, aimed his laser gauntlet, squeezed his fist and the four laser fingers lashed out knifing into Mekahn, killing him. Harper, nearby, witnessed the death of her old love's worst enemy and was glad for him. Their eyes met and they exchanged an expression that said so.

In front of the portal, Katch was sweating, trembling now. "I can't hold it." Aliena's concentration had broken as well. The platform no longer rocked and the crystal started to dissolve into existence again. The machine hummed and the ray stabbed out devastating a group of Enchantment and rebel forces. Garrum were also caught by it. Of course, to Karayahn, they were just collateral damage.

Katch slumped to his knees, exhausted. Merlin was still weakened by his wound. Aliena knew that now had to be her moment. If she was ever going to become her intended self, the final outcome was up to the warrior, the strong leader she had become. She rushed forward to grab the reins of a riderless horse nearby, quickly mounted and rode through the hell of battle toward the death machine. Her spinning laser knives were useful to down anyone trying to stop her, including a Garrum Guard who lost a hand while attempting to grab the reins of her horse. Within a few yards of the starcrystal, Aliena dismounted, walking over the now blood-soaked soil to stand as close as she dared to her formidable enemy.

Karayahn noticed the small, auburn-haired woman, seemingly the only being standing rock still midst the movement of hand-to-hand combat all around her. This had to be the rebel leader, the Aregnan songsayer Aliena; the last of the despised family who had always been such a force in her life. The two locked eyes without blinking. It was as if the battle around them was surreal, a swirling, crimson blur and there were only these two, very different adversaries left alive.

Karayahn snapped out of it and screamed to her techno-wizard minions on the platform. The Crystal had now firmly reappeared. "Turn it! Their leader, that little hell-bitch is there!" She pointed toward Aliena who still stood her ground, her brow wrinkling as she summoned the courage and concentration to fully use her powers.

Spotting Aliena standing frozen in place while Garrum, on foot, were getting way too close to her, Beige, with Harper now at his side, rushed forward to keep them busy. What the hell was she doing? Did the woman have a sudden death wish?

With the dreaded starcrystal weapon almost lined up to blast her way, Aliena used the same gesture Greer used as she concentrated on her enemy with all her angry power. It was instinctual now. Karayahn was hit and staggered by an invisible force. She gasped in shock, tried to recover and was hit again. The techno-wizards stared at the Grand Magician unable to see what was causing her to stumble. Beige froze a bit himself after downing a Garrum and smiled. Oh, his little general had a death wish alright...but not for herself.

Aliena gestured again and Karayahn started to scream as she was attacked over and over by the power of Aliena Aregnan's long-dormant Psychokinesis. Each "shove" pushed her closer to the ray! "Fire you idiots! Destroy her. Now!" The techno-wizards fired but, simultaneously, Aliena's mental attack shoved the Grand Magician in front of the beam. Lycenia Karayahn's last shriek was cut short by her fall to the ground as a long log of steaming, distorted flesh, transformed beyond all human recognition.

Still in control and fiercely concentrating, Aliena gestured again and the Machine started to swing around, the ray raised to miss rebel and Enchantment forces and leveled on the techno-wizard ranks. Those atop the Crystal platform lept off and ran. As the beam started to cut into them, the remaining techno-wizards and Garrum broke off fighting and also deserted. The rebels and Enchantment army chased after them, taking prisoners and routing the rest.

Merlin was able to raise the top half of his body a little and sent his own gentle psychic message to Aliena. "You can stop now, your Highness. It is done."

She "heard", sighed and relaxed, finally releasing her control and falling to her knees, exhausted. The starcrystal machine stopped and whined down but Aliena looked into the distance and shook her head. She mentally responded. "Not quite yet, Merle. Look to the North." He turned to face North and saw that Modred was spurring his horse away with Arthur in fast pursuit. "That is an old score still to be settled, I think", she thought. Merlin produced a grim smile and said aloud, "You have no idea."

Chapter 23

Arthur carried his beloved Excalibur unsheathed and bloody in his hand as he galloped ahead chasing his longtime nemesis while yelling. "Face me Modred!"

Modred only spurred his horse harder. As Arthur yelled his name over and over, Modred ignored the call to a fair fight. Finally, in anguish, Arthur hurled the trusted blade at his retreating enemy. It sailed gracefully though the air, sparkling in the golden, late day light and imbedded itself in Modred's back.

Modred fell heavily to the ground as his horse galloped on. Arthur reined in, dismounted and kneeled at his side.

"Your betrayals are never ending but you could have faced me."

With his death rattle, "I could never face you. I am who I am. You know that." His cough brought up a trickle of blood. Bet you are sorry you let me out of that glass coffin."

"I had hope for you nephew."

Modred managed a small smile. "Silly king". He stiffened and died. Arthur bowed his head for a beat. Why did it have to end this way? Part of him couldn't believe his long struggle with this now ancient enemy had finally ended. Modred's lifeless eyes were open. Arthur put forth a gentle hand and closed them. Clouds had rolled in and it had begun to rain. Arthur slowly straightened, recovered Excalibur and led his horse to the nearby battlefield where the techno-wizards and Garrum still alive were being herded together into makeshift prisoner compounds. Any able to walk who were reluctant were herded by Yaustis and his fellow hweens with a light brush of many wings and powerful tails. The surviving rebels and most of the Enchantment army searched among their own for wounded they could aid. Rain was washing the blood of battle from the field.

A bit later, Harper and Katch were up on the platform checking out the now dead machine. "I think this thing's burnt out", said Harper while patting it.

"I bet Aliena cracked the crystal", Katch replied with pride. Padraig joined them while Harper strolled around the once deadly techno marvel reflecting. "It would have been nice to see what good we could have done with it. I never saw a crystal like that though".

Padraig laughed. "That? It's lying all over the ground on our side of the portals. The Grand Magician over there…", he indicated the malformed, charred mass that was once the ruler of the realm, "would have used crystals to power weapons but our young ones use them for games of, I think you call it, marbles." Katch and Harper exchanged a look. Harper moved closer to Padraig. "Any chance of making a trade? We've got some real nice agates on this side."

Padraig's hand explored the burned-out crystal remains. "I don't see why not, It's of no use to us but it might do some earthly good for you people."

Midst survivors looking for wounded comrades, Arthur and Merlin found each other. The ancient wizard had recovered enough to be mobile. Merlin noticed the gore and blood dripping from Excalibur. "Your old friend has been busy."

The two sat down on nearby boulders. "Excalibur is a mixed blessing. To have it in my hands again feels...right but wielding it against a very old enemy was somehow very difficult."

Merlin leaned forward. "Modred."

Arthur wiped the blood from his beloved sword. "Yes. There has never been true hope that he would change, that his lust for power and control would simply vanish one day but I suppose I foolishly hoped that, in this new land..." He bowed his head. "He wouldn't face me you know."

Merlin put a reassuring hand on his long-time pupil's blood-soaked arm. "It has ended as it had to, as it was, perhaps pre-destined." Arthur nodded. "I know."

Arthur stood and walked heavily back to the Tinabulon Portal where Aliena, having regained her strength, now stood looking out over the field as the dead were being gathered. The bodies of Jobie and Jorn had been discovered and had been carried by Stellar and Wolfer to lie near the portal.

Harper was now talking with a sad Devlin who held the reins of Strongheart as she fixed her eyes on Jobie's body. The horse moved closer to the small young woman and nuzzled her, seeming to indeed recognize his human friend and her sorrow. Beige, Shang-Sui, Tiberius, Yaustis, and other survivors including Stellar, Wolfer and Aaron, looking the worse for battle wear, stood nearby. Arthur still carried Excalibur unsheathed in his hand and now started to put it back in his scabbard. Before he could complete the motion, Aliena dropped to her knees before him. "Your majesty."

Arthur hadn't heard this greeting in a very long while. "What?"

Aliena, songsayer, battle general, last of a ruling family looked up at a King. "When I saw how your sword was returned to you, I knew who you were. Not Artos, a soldier on the wander, but Arthur, the King Who did Not Die. I've sung your song often enough to know."

"That was a long time ago." Arthur replied as all those around him stared in awe. He sighed, relieved that his secret was finally revealed.

Aliena continued. "You were to come to us when most we needed you and you did. Your line is far older than mine, Sire…and this kingdom is still yours to command."

Arthur reached down, grasped Aliena's hands firmly in his and raised her to her feet.

"My time is past, girl. You are the rightful ruler of this realm."

Her self-doubt was front and center. "But I'm not trained for it. I've always been a songsayer…"

He thought back to his own beginnings. "If you remember the legend, I wasn't trained for it either, except by Merlin. I dare say he's still a good teacher."

"But I can't."

"Of course you can."

He led her over toward the milling, victorious rebels on the field and raised his booming voice. "Hear me, people!"

They turned toward Arthur and Aliena curiously.

"The dictator, so-called Grand Magician is dead. Her underlings and troops are defeated, dead or running."

The crowd cheered and he waved them quiet. He turned Aliena forward to face her subjects.

"I give you the Princess Elector, Aliena, last of the House of Aregnan, rightful heir of the throne of this land."

Then he drew Excalibur, kneeled, took her hand and placed it on the hilt. He then covered her small hand with his as the rebels cheered mightily. Aliena hesitated then firmly grasped the hilt as her eyes locked with Arthur's.

Beige watched intently. There was something between these two that was stronger than anything he could ever offer the "little general". His days of competing for her attention had to be put to rest. He felt eyes on his neck. He turned to find his old flame Harper behind him.

She'd been watching the warm exchange between royalty as tears glistened slightly in her eyes. He smiled. She smiled back. No snarky comments? There might still be something here after all...or maybe not. Devlin was looking at her much as he had often looked at Aliena.

A few days later, rebel forces gathered in the courtyard of what had been the Grand Magician's stronghold and the seat of the former and now current Aregnan rule. All were in somber mood and dressed in dark colors. All eyes were locked on the center of the courtyard where fallen warrior Foresters Jorn and Jobie, dressed in their best, were lying atop a high funeral pyre. One tall and wiry and the other short and stocky, they were an odd "couple". Jorn's long, blonde hair was neatly braided and lay over his right shoulder.

Beige, wearing his best old and still impressive Forester clothes, stepped up to stand in front of the pyre. At a short distance, Aliena and Arthur, with Merlin and Katch by their sides, looked quite regal in rich, dark robes. Devlin and Harper, wearing long, flattering dresses for a change, stood behind them. Padraig and Tiberius, resplendent in their Enchantment best, were nearby while Yaustis curled to lie down near a lovely old oak tree where he could view the proceedings.

Prominent at a distance from the pyre, the Foresters were lined up facing Beige. A closer examination would have revealed silent tears rolling down many a rugged cheek as Beige cleared his throat and spoke.

"Brothers and sisters in arms, we are here to celebrate the lives of two of our Forester band fallen in battle. They fought gallantly. Jorn put himself between me and a Garrum arrowlock missile and I am forever in his debt. Jobie, who could stealthily lift a purse from the belt of any being who ever lived, took down an enemy cavalryman but, before he could rise, our brother was killed by another despite Devlin's brave efforts to fight off several Garrum."

Foresters smiled at the reference to Jobie's pickpocketing skills but Devlin began to cry at remembering the Forester's last moments. How did she fail to save him? She curled against Harper who pulled her close trying to comfort. In the process, Harper's hand touched the scalloped top of one of the young woman's ears. The hand moved in a slight caress.

Beige, with difficulty, continued. "We give them our highest tribute." He walked further from the pyre to join the line of Foresters, took his bow from his shoulder, withdrew the Calling Arrow from its quiver, leaned back, nocked it and aimed for the pyre. "We call the souls of our fallen brothers to join us. You live in our hearts. We will never forget you." The other Foresters had set fire to the tips of their arrows but the Calling Arrow created its own unique fire.

Beige let go the special arrow and it flashed and produced a glowing trail like a comet until it landed high near the top of the pyre and, still flashing, lit the first flame. Wolfer nocked his burning arrow and fired immediately after, followed by Stellar then Aaron and the rest of the Foresters until all arrows had hit their marks and the pyre was completely ablaze.

Aliena, lyrit in hand, stepped forward to sing her own composition, a tribute to the two warrior Foresters that brought more tears to many an eye. The sad congregation then watched in silence until the bodies of their two comrades in arms were finally engulfed and destroyed by the flames.

After a moment, Wolfer sniffed, wiped a tear, slowly turned to Beige, slapped his shoulder and announced. "The boys and I are headed to the nearest tavern to toast Jobie and Jorn. Are you with us?" Beige shouldered his bow again, looked a last time at the pyre then, "What do you think? Lead the way. Let's ask Harper to join us." Wolfer nodded in approval. Beige turned in Harper's direction, about to yell her name but saw that she and a still upset Devlin were slowly walking away arm-in-arm. He cracked a toothy smile. Oh, so that's how it was.

Chapter 24

A week later, Aliena, clad in a long, flattering royal purple dress that complimented her auburn hair and wearing an understated crown, entered the first council chamber where the rebellion was born. She was followed by Arthur, Merlin, Padraig, Tiberius, Yaustis, Beige and Katch. Beige stepped forward. "Uh, your highness, there's a stack of papers on the desk I should be attending to."

Aliena smiled. "Of course, Connery. Go on about your business." He bowed and walked away putting an arm around a pretty, statuesque, blonde woman who willingly went with him. "Who is that?", Aliena raised an eyebrow and inquired. "Wolfer's sister, up from the forest province", Arthur replied. "See how he follows to keep an eye on her." Indeed, Wolfer was following the couple, at a respectable but chaperoning distance.

Aliena smiled. Beige would ever be the flirt. "You know, I think Connery actually enjoys administering the kingdom although I'm sure he and his Foresters will ride again...on the right side of the law this time. It's in their blood. But I still need good generals. The remaining techno-wizards and Garrum could still cause more trouble."

He knew she was launching her campaign for him to stay. "Wolfer has taken over Connery's command most ably."

Padraig stepped forward. "And you can always count on us." He pulled a plett from his pocket. "In fact, the Enchantment would like you to have this Tinabulon Portal key. We know that it's symbolic only. You can open our gates with your mind." He bowed, offered it and she gracefully took it, replying, "I would never be so rude as to pick the lock like that. I will wait for an invitation." Padraig bowed again gracefully. "Come to visit any time. You are welcomed."

Tiberius shrugged. "Sure. You'll be treated like the royal folk you are…if we can roust the Mid-Eve Council out again."

Yaustis was lying down in order to fit comfortably in the lower-ceilinged room. "Since our Gentry learned that their Elders spirited Arthur away and used their technology and magic to keep him in the cave against the time when both our worlds would be in danger, I think they're more in tune with this RealWorld now. They were happy to gather an army to help save it."

"And we are most grateful", Aliena bowed. "We will certainly stay in touch. I want to know much more about how our people can cooperate." She nodded to Padraig. "Thank you." She pocketed the plett.

Merlin smiled addressing Padraig and Yaustis. "Your people have our endless gratitude for preserving our king. Their talents were of great use."

Arthur nodded. "And will be again."

Aliena looked surprised and worried. "Again? Surely you know we need you still. Stay and help me govern. We can take the old machines Karayahn used for evil, power them up with crystals from our Enchantment friends and use them the right way…to help our people."

"Your people", Arthur emphasized. "Merle, uh Merlin will stay to assist with the machines. As for governing, it's better to let your own good sense and kind heart guide you."

She moved closer. "But you could help so much." He leaned forward and spoke gently. "Aliena, I did what I was destined to do. But I am out of place in your world. I believe I must return to the cave and wait in sleep should I be needed again."

He pulled her to him gently and embraced her lightly as he kissed her cheek. She wanted so much more but he put her from him, bowed quickly and walked away. Aliena didn't see him close his eyes and frown after struggling with his difficult decision. Merlin watched this with a jaundiced eye. Katch could see and sense his sister's deep sadness. As Arthur left, Merlin, still grimacing a bit due to his battle wound, came to Aliena's side. She turned her back, fighting tears, affected deeply by this awful loss. Katch moved closer. He didn't like seeing her so upset.

"Arthur always was pig stubborn", confided Merlin. "He also has a very deeply-ingrained sense of duty. You'll have to forgive me, because I was the one who impressed it on him." The old magician heaved a deep sigh.

"I understand, Merlin. I just hate so to lose him."

Katch shrugged his shoulders. "She loves him." Only a 10-year-old could be so blunt about matters of the heart. Aliena was embarrassed. "Katch! Please."

As Merlin suspected, there was more than friendship, gratitude and comradery here. "Truly, your highness?"

She turned to face him revealing the flowing tears she could fight no longer.

Soon after, inside the cave where Arthur and Modred awoke what seemed now to be an eon ago, the Once and Future King's cryogenic tank was closed and his vague nude form could be seen as he slept inside it. Excalibur rested at his side. Around the cave the technical mechanisms that maintained the tank busily winked and worked. Suddenly, the lid of the sarcophagus lifted. Arthur's eyes slowly opened. He sat up, looking around warily. Aliena stepped forward from the shadows, chin held high. "Arthur."

He shook his head to clear it. "How did you get here? What have you done?"

She moved closer. "Merlin told me how to awaken you again." She handed him a garment made of lightweight leather. "Uh, pants." She turned aside as he climbed from his resting place and put them on.

He sadly shook his head. "No. Aliena, I cannot…"

She took his hand. "You didn't listen to the legend, Arthur. It said you'd ride forth when we needed you most. It didn't say anything about going back. This world needs you. I need you. Can you leave us so easily?"

Arthur studied her for a long time, seeing the need and the love in her face. He could no longer deny that he felt the same. "It's a strange world you've called me into, Aliena. But no…I can't leave it. Or <u>you</u>."

Then, he pulled her into his arms for a very warm and close embrace. They clung desperately to each other and he kissed her, finally…long and thoroughly until both felt transported to an exciting but warm and safe haven. A bit breathless, she tipped her head back a little to look into his eyes, smiled up at him then helped him walk outside on his only slightly shaky legs.

"There's a red ring around the moon, Arthur…and they say legends are born on nights like this." They embraced again then looked toward this future Earth's horizon as the rising, debris-ringed moon, again cast its strange glow on the twisted, jagged peaks of the distant mountain range.

The moonlight revealed toppled, once towering ruins of a civilization that existed…long ago. His eyes on them, Arthur could almost see even farther into the past, to another, much older realm in which idealistic knights and their even more idealistic king sat around a circular table. The moon's shimmering red ring made for an eerie sight that could be foreboding to the average eye but Arthur was beginning to appreciate it. Besides, there was much to do here and, with the extraordinary Aliena at his side, he knew he could accomplish miracles.

THE END

BIOGRAPHY

D.C. Fontana

D.C. Fontana (1939-2019) was one of very few female scribes to write action adventure television in the 1960's. After writing for several Western genre shows ("Bonanza", "Big Valley" among others), she was best known for developing the half Vulcan, half human character Mr. Spock of "Star Trek" fame and story editing the original series plus writing, story editing and associate producing the "Next Generation" and "Star Trek Animated" series. Her multi-genre T.V. credits are too plentiful to list here and she wrote scripts for several video games. Dorothy's prose work was published by Simon and Schuster, Ballantine, Morrow and others.

Lynn Barker wrote scripts for the 1980's reboot of "The Twilight Zone". Other WGA T.V. credits include "Star Trek: Deep Space Nine" and "Amazing Stories". Her articles have appeared in "American Cinematographer" and the WGA magazine "Written By:" and she has a story in the "Chicken Soup for the Soul of America" book. Lynn worked as Story Department Manager for the CBS Television Network and was an MPAA-accredited Hollywood entertainment journalist for several websites. Writing experience also includes show and pre-show scripts for Disney Imagineering and Universal theme park attractions. She is a script doctor and screenplay consultant.

FUTURUS REX

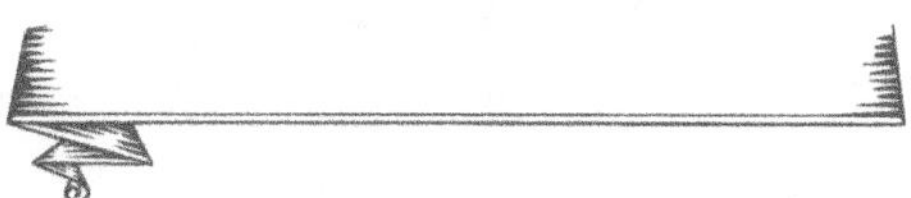

Novel by Lynn Barker/D.C. Fontana, based upon a screenplay by Lynn Barker, D.C. Fontana, and Budd Lewis. Cover art by Budd Lewis. "A Star to Steer By" music and lyrics by Karen Willson, © 1978.